nonfiction

a novel

julie myerson

corsair

CORSAIR

First published in the UK in 2022 by Corsair

1 3 5 7 9 10 8 6 4 2

All characters and events in this publication, other than those clearly in the public domain, are fictitious and any resemblance to real persons, living or dead, is purely coincidental.

A CIP catalogue record for this book is available from the British Library.

ISBN: 978-1-4721-5677-8

Typeset in Bembo by M Rules
Printed and bound in Great Britain by
Clays Ltd, Elcograf S.p.A.

Papers used by Corsair are from well-managed forests and other responsible sources.

MIX
Paper from responsible sources
FSC
FSC® C104740

Corsair
An imprint of
Book Group
Carmelite House
An Hachette UK Company
www.littlebrown.co.uk

nonfiction

One

THERE'S A NIGHT – I THINK this is the middle of June – when we lock you in the house. We don't want to do it, but – or so we tell each other – we seem to have no choice. In those days we rarely go out, any kind of social activity has begun to seem pointless, but for some reason I no longer remember we don't want to miss this dinner. So we lock all the doors and leave you with a hammer, so you can smash a window in case of fire. Your father doesn't think this is necessary, but I think it's necessary. I don't want you to die in a fire. Or, I don't want to have to sit through a dinner party on the other side of town, while all the time worrying that you might die in a fire.

I know, of course I do, that it makes no sense – to

leave you locked in there while still armed with the means of escape. I know it's entirely possible, given the state of mind you're in, that you might start a fire just so you can have a reason to smash the window. It wouldn't be the first time you've taken such a risk, damaging property or possessions simply in order to get your way. It is, let's face it, exactly the kind of reckless trick you are capable of pulling back then.

But I have to admit that you don't do that. You make no attempt at all to get out. You microwave the dinner we leave for you and you rinse the plate and put it in the dishwasher and then, after watching something on your laptop, you go up to bed.

When we return, the house is silent. Nothing seems to be missing or damaged. No money has been taken. The hammer is exactly where we left it on the table in the hall. You do not appear to have made any attempt to break the glass.

I AM SURE THAT ONE DAY when things are better your father and I will look back on these days with disbelief. I hope that we will. For now, though, we take each separate incident in our stride, behaving, to each other anyway, as if this life of ours is normal, as if it's exactly the kind of life that everyone lives.

Time blurs when you are dealing with chaos. Everything blurs. We too, sometimes, are a blur. Each morning we wake to a brand new day and we just get on with it, transforming ourselves into whatever shape or form is necessary in order to deal with whatever chaos or disaster comes next.

So many things which pass for normal in our house: the windows broken, the cups and plates smashed, the doors kicked in. The visits to A&E, the police being called. The times when one of us will, almost without a second thought, rush to hide the block of kitchen knives in the cupboard under the stairs. Or take the house keys from their hook by the door and fling them under a cushion on the sofa.

The fact that I always hide my bag the moment I come home and your father would never dream of leaving his jacket or trousers lying around with money in them. The anger and the anguish and the shouting, the things I no longer dare to do or say. The dreams and plans I've ceased to find it in me to care about, the pleasures we've forgotten to take.

The moments when we have no idea what's coming next, what violence or drama or deceit, when we can't imagine what new bad thing might lie around the corner.

The jagged, upset evenings when I admit we find it very hard indeed to calm down.

The days when my first thought on waking is: I don't know if I can go on like this.

The nights when we talk and shout and weep and

then, as if nothing at all has happened, we sit and eat dinner in front of the news before putting ourselves to bed, where we sleep like babies simply because there's no energy left in our hearts to keep us awake.

ON THE DAY THAT YOUR father goes with you on the train to the place where you're going to stay for three months (we tell you three but, I can admit it now, both of us are very much hoping it will be longer), I take you to the chemist for the very last time. As usual we queue outside with the others, but this time I allow myself a quick moment of satisfaction – or perhaps it's relief – at the thought that tomorrow they will still be here and you and I will not.

After that, we cross the road to the bus stop. You have a large nylon rucksack which we bought you especially for the trip, as well as an old black duffel bag belonging to your father. Ever since you were a child you've been mysteriously in love with this bag, always begging to borrow it – it used to accompany you everywhere, swimming and on sleepovers and on school trips – so it seems only right that it should go with you now.

As usual, your dirty old bashed-up guitar case is slung over your shoulder. (When we query the guitar, you insist that the woman you spoke to at the centre said it was OK. But this turns out not to be the case, and when you arrive with it she isn't at all pleased and your father has to bring it all the way back with him on the train.)

Now, standing at the bus stop, your father checks to see when the bus is coming. Two minutes away, he says. One minute. He glances up at the street.

One minute.

I reach for you. Putting my arms around you, feeling the smallness of your rib cage, the way your bones move and crunch like the bones of a baby bird. Your shoulders are hunched, your almost non-existent breasts caving beneath your ragged T-shirt. There's the faintest odour of sweat. When I draw away, I catch the familiar, musty scent of your breath. Your eyes are huge.

I ask you if you're nervous. No, you say, you aren't nervous, you're ready. All you want right now, you say, is to get on with it.

Good, I say, That's good. That's the exact right attitude to have – and then I tell you that I love you so much – that we both love you. And – though I know I've begun to say it a few too many times in the past however many days – I tell you again how proud we both are, that you've managed to come this far. Whatever happens next, you did this. Remember that, I tell you –

Yeah, well, you say.

You put your ear buds in.

And you get on the bus, the two of you, your father taking the card back off you as soon as you've touched in. I watch as you stand there together at the foot of the stairs and then your father gives a little wave and the bus goes around the corner and is gone.

I WALK HOME SLOWLY, TAKING my time, because suddenly what reason is there to rush? It's a beautiful day, the sun shining and the light perfect, bright and hot – in fact I have to admit that everything is pretty perfect now, for we have every reason to believe that you'll stay in that place for at least three months, and with a bit of luck perhaps even longer. Even the worst case scenario means that we get to have the summer off. Long days and evenings of being normal, of eating and sleeping and dealing with ordinary, everyday problems. Even, it begins to dawn on me, the possibility of having some fun.

I could go shopping for clothes. Get my hair cut. Meet a friend for coffee. We could even see what's on at the cinema.

Odd, then, to find that I don't feel very free at all. The opposite, actually. I feel hemmed in, on edge, angry and defiant, my whole body tense and defended, as if I've been accused of something.

Perhaps I have been accused of something.

Walking through the market, I catch myself clenching my fists, irritated by all these people dawdling so benignly along with their bags and their dogs and their pushchairs, picking up this thing or that thing, going about their business with such maddening ease on this perfect summer's day.

A woman with a large and complicated pushchair stops right there in the middle of the pavement to take a call. Her phone in one hand, a carton of juice in the other, the child kicking and flinging its limbs angrily around while she chats on and people are forced to part to make their way around her.

I watch as she throws her head back and laughs, handing the juice to her infant so that she can gesticulate with her free hand before slowly moving on.

Back home, closing the front door, silence blooms around me. For the past several weeks, we've been forced to act as your jailers – we knew it would be foolish to trust you, you said you didn't want us to trust you – and so we've stuck close by you, both of us, we've watched your every step. Every plan, every moment, has been accounted for. Recently, you've never once left this house without one of us in tow.

It feels very disconcerting, then, to walk in here alone.

In a minute, I'll go up to your room and begin cleaning it. I'll remove all the dirty plates and mouldy drinks and put all of the rubbish – most of which I'll find on the floor or under your bed – into bin bags. I'll scrape chewing gum off the floorboards and fish cigarette filters out from behind the radiator. I'll hoover the brown tobacco flakes off the tops of the books – picture books and pop-up books and annuals and encyclopaedias – most of which (and yes, I admit this does give me pain every time I think of it) have been on the shelf in that room ever since you were a baby.

After that, I'll change the sheets – adding the quilted counterpane we had dry-cleaned long ago, but have kept in its polythene, waiting for the moment when we can safely return this room to a state of innocence. But first – just because I can – I hang my bag, along with all of my money, bank cards and keys, up on the hooks in the hall.

YOUR FATHER ASKS ME IF I KNOW that my mother is a bully. Not like other mothers, he says, not just thoughtless or difficult or overdemanding or trampling all over their children's feelings through a lack of tact or oversight. No, he says, your mother is actively cruel. She knows what she's doing, she thinks it through. Can't you see that she actually goes out of her way to do you harm?

Can I see it? Do I know it? Do I? What I do know is that what my mother wants, more than anything – more probably even than the normal pleasures and satisfactions of life – is for things to go wrong for me. I know that she would like to see me fail, to come a cropper (her words), to end up hating myself, to sink right down to some mysterious place of darkness and shame, just so that she can say: I told you so – just so that she can be proved right.

I also know that when things begin to go wrong with you – our beloved, our once bright and sweet and happy child – it seems to give her a special kind of satisfaction. It's right there on her face, in her voice, her eyes, in her frequent phone calls which are more and more full of ridicule and anger and more and more noticeably devoid of any tenderness.

All the same, she is my mother and I admit I get a small, tight pain in my chest when I hear your father say these things.

Though who can blame him. Over the years he's had to endure the very worst of her. From the first moment she meets him – over lunch in a dark city restaurant two years before you are born – her dislike is instant. Remaining silent and seated as she shakes his hand, looking him up and down, and sitting there with her bracelets and her cigarette lighter, expectant and ungiving, as she waits for him to ask her all about herself.

And when he doesn't do that – when, in the first of so many fatal mistakes, he treats her just like any normal person, smiling and laughing, but also daring to chat about something other than the simple fact of how remarkable she is – she shivers and, with a glint of satisfaction, or perhaps it is fury, in her eyes, she reaches for her jacket and pulls it around her shoulders.

Taking a breath, looking around her, asking the

waiter to please bring her a glass of water. Taking out her cigarettes and placing them on the table next to her, even though she can't smoke them yet. Pushing away her glass of wine, even though I know she would prefer to finish it.

And that's it, after that, she doesn't bother again – her face is stiff, it is ice – it is downhill all the way after that.

When we say our goodbyes, she pulls me to her – urgently, hungrily – as if she expects never to see me again. Be careful, she says – gripping my elbows with her fingers, her mouth a hard, tight line. You take very good care of yourself, won't you, my darling?

Yes, my mother is a bully.

AFTER SHE DIES, WHEN SHE'S gone, but does not seem to be gone – I tell your father that I can't be left alone at home, not for the whole night anyway.

The day's all right, I can cope with the day – though now that I think about it, the very last time it happened was in broad and brilliant daylight – but if he has a late meeting in the city, he mustn't accept any invitations to stay over, he must be very sure to get the last train back.

I don't care what time you get back as long as I know you are coming, I say, trying not to listen to myself because I know how it sounds.

And when, standing there in the doorway with his

briefcase in his hands, he asks me what exactly it is that I am afraid of, I tell him I can't put it into words.

Try?

He is waiting. His face is kind, his voice patient, attentive.

I just can't.

I know that your father thinks that these days I am half the person I used to be, that I'm not the person he married, not that girl who strode around and laughed and did all kinds of brave and funny things and wasn't afraid of the dark.

He's not wrong about this. I think it too.

ON THE DAY THAT I TELL MY mother that I might be leaving your father, she can't hide her delight. I've never seen her so lit up and attentive and alive. Perhaps she sees a whole new future opening up in front of us, maybe she imagines that I'll shrink right back to being a child again, hers to guide and manage as she wants. But when, a few months later, I tell her we're giving it another go, that in my heart I think I still love him, this man who I have after all spent most of my adult life with, that for the sake of our child, our marriage is surely worth fighting for, her eyes empty. It's clear that she has nothing to say.

It's the exact same look she has on her face when we tell her – with relief and fear and excitement – that you've at last agreed to come home and let us help you. Even though by then she knows very well the full horror of what's been happening, even though she knows how very bad things have been for you, how terrified we both are, still she can't seem to bring herself to say anything. Grasping that there's no way for her to influence the situation and – perhaps especially – that there's nothing in it for her, she remains silent. After a moment or two, she lights a cigarette and then she changes the subject.

There's another day, too. A day when, having tried for weeks to find you, and having no idea of where you are or even if you are safe, I sit with my mother in a cafe round the corner from her home and – crying into a bunch of paper napkins – tell her how I cannot sleep or eat, how all I can think about is whether you're OK.

I have these visions, I tell her, of you lying alone somewhere, in some alley or ditch or squalid crack-house bedroom, dead or ill or overdosing or bleeding and harmed.

I know that these outcomes are pretty unlikely – that the most likely thing is you've found some stoner's sofa to sleep on – but all the same I can't stop the visions from coming.

I tell her how very worthless I feel, how much of a failure – such a terrible failure of a mother, unable to protect or even speak to my child. With tears in my eyes, I confide to her that I do not mind if you never want to see me again, fair enough – I've thought a lot about it and I believe I could live with that, I say. I don't actually need anything from you, my daughter. All I need, I tell my mother, is to know that you are safe and well and alive, that you still have a calm and happy life ahead of you, that you will live.

As I try to explain all of these things to her, I can't stop crying. Even though there are plenty of people in the cafe and some of them are looking at us, even though I understand that my sobbing like this in a public place isn't a good thing to do, that it's needlessly dramatic and ugly and embarrassing, still I can't help it, I can't seem to do anything about it, I can't stop.

I cry so much that in the end I have to get up and fetch more napkins from the place beside the till.

And through all of this, my mother says nothing. Sitting there very calmly, the newspaper with its loud and ranting headlines folded neatly beside her, her foaming coffee half-drunk. Watching me with a mild kind of curiosity on her face, as if she doesn't really know me all that well – as if she's never properly seen me before – at last she brushes the shortbread crumbs from her lap and tells me that in her view I should try and pull myself together and get on with things.

She doesn't mean to be harsh, she says – and of course she understands that this might not be what I want to hear – but it's the only bit of advice she has for me at present, just get on with it, she says.

And at the time, this does seem reasonable.

But later – many months later when you're back in our lives and a lot has changed both for good and for bad but the world is, briefly anyway, ordinary again – I discover that on that day I met my mother at the cafe, you were at her house all along.

Just around the corner from where I was sitting, right there in her house, only a matter of metres away, you were, at that moment, probably still in bed.

You'd been there at least a week, it turned out. This was why my mother hadn't called me on the Sunday night as she usually did, why she'd seemed reluctant to invite me to the house. At the time I hadn't questioned this, but looking back she'd been very firm about it. The cafe's so much nicer, she'd said.

She had sat there and watched me crying for at least an hour and in all that time she'd known exactly where you were and she'd said nothing.

Your father's even more shocked by this than I am. Years later, he still refers to it, saying he considers such behaviour to be inhuman, wicked even. To be capable of witnessing your child's distress and to have it in your power to soothe her and yet to refuse to do so. He says it tells you everything you need to know about my mother.

But I don't know –

I don't know what it tells me.

I see people walking around arm in arm with their

mothers, talking and laughing, as if nothing is all that difficult and the whole of life is one great big warm joke and I look at them and I realise that after all this time alive in the world, I know nothing.

I GO TO A MEETING. YOUR father won't come, he doesn't think he needs to. He's only just got back from work, he says he has better things to do with his evening. And we've been in this situation for long enough that I know not to force it. It's a warm evening, the air loud with birdsong, the kind of evening when normal people might relax in their gardens or stand outside a pub and laugh and drink. Instead I park the car and take myself into the cool gloom of a church crypt, where seven or eight people are already sitting around a table and a woman is shaking biscuits onto a plate.

I've seen most of the people before, but there's a new man, middle-aged, slim and unshaven, with a tense look on his face. And when the prayers have been read and we've all been around and said who we are, he tells us, in a slow and halting voice – almost as if he too is hearing it for the very first time – what it is that happened with his son.

How the mother of one of his son's friends, someone they'd never even met, went round to the place where their boy was living, a place which he and his wife had (admittedly against their better judgement) been paying the rent on. And how she had the absolutely terrible job of phoning them.

The poor woman.

I would not wish that job on anyone, he says. He's thought about it a lot, actually, in the months since it happened. She should never even have been there – if you think about it, it was just pure chance that she happened to be the one. Her daughter wasn't even a very close friend of their son's, just someone he'd once known from school. But she'd been round to see him recently and she'd left a jacket there and this woman had apparently been passing and the daughter had asked if she could pop in and get it for her.

She rang the bell but no one answered. But the door was slightly open and so she called out, and when nothing happened she went on in.

He hesitates. Around the table, nobody moves.

He was cooking, he says, when he took the call. Trying to get the dinner on – he gives a little laugh. And this woman, she sounded very distressed, and she explained straightaway that before she'd done anything else, she'd called an ambulance, that they'd said they were on their way, but she told him that –

Her voice was very hard to hear between the sobs.

For some reason which he still doesn't understand, he did not panic, not at all. Very calmly, before he did anything else, he turned off the gas on the hob. He turned off the oven too. He thinks – and he lets out another small laugh as he says this – he may even have drained the peas.

He isn't sure if he drained the peas.

Certainly, he pulled out a chair, sat down. He even heard himself trying to comfort the poor woman – she really was in the most terrible state – telling her that what she needed to do right now was take some breaths, to try and calm herself down.

Gazing at the floor, he sighs. He says he doesn't know what else to tell us. It's been five months now. Five months and frankly it's not getting any easier. He's wondering if it ever gets easier – he knows he's not the only one but seriously, can anyone here tell him, does it ever get any easier?

Someone, the woman sitting next to him, places a hand on his sleeve. And he looks at this hand for a very long moment, considering it with a genuinely curious expression on his face, as if it might tell him something.

At last he lets out a sigh.

The funny thing was, he really was the sweetest, brightest, happiest, most loving child, no problem at all when he was young.

And he lifts his head and looks around the room. As if he's waiting for someone to tell him what happens next.

WHEN YOU WEEP AND FUME and shout at us, we tell ourselves that it's all just part of growing up. Mornings when, aged twelve or thirteen, you lie yourself down on the rug in the hall and refuse to go to school and – busy, stressed, running late – we pull you to your feet and tell you to stop being so dramatic and then, having seen you off, we watch from the window to make sure you're heading up towards the tube.

I think of you now in that packed train carriage with your rucksack and your ratty, early morning hair and tear-stained face and all of your many difficulties and sorrows and the flat raw fact of who you are and aren't at that time and my heart just breaks.

How could we have done that to you?

How could I?

And there's a night when you are older – maybe fourteen or fifteen – when I come home very late and find you sitting all alone in the dark at the kitchen table, playing with the short sharp knife we use for cutting lemons. Turning it around and around in your hands, testing the blade against your fingers. Looking up now and then to check my face, as you press the sharp pointed tip against your soft flesh.

I don't panic. I'm supremely steady in those days, still hopeful, I suppose, still unscarred.

Taking off my coat and throwing it over the chair, I tell you to put the knife down. The moment you do it, I slip it back in the block where it belongs, just as if it's nothing, as if it's entirely normal for you to play with knives. Switching on the small light on the dresser, making the room safe and homely again, I make you a hot drink and we talk about other things – I think we even make each other laugh –

And that's that, I don't give it another thought.

I don't do what surely most parents would do and wake up sweating in the middle of the night and think: a knife.

Another time I'm sitting in a restaurant many miles from home, eating dinner after some book event or other, and my phone rings and it's you and you say that you want to ask me something. But your voice sounds funny, not at all like your normal voice, and the line keeps on breaking up and it's hard to tell if you are laughing or crying.

These are the days when it would not for a single moment occur to me to ask you if you're high.

I tell you it's hard to talk in the restaurant. More of a pub really, the place is packed and I have to keep my hand clamped to my ear just to catch a single word of what you're saying. I ask you if you're OK and I don't know what you say, but you must tell me that you are OK, because I know that we establish that it isn't any kind of an emergency and I say goodbye to you, I tell you I'll speak to you tomorrow.

You are fourteen, maybe fifteen years old. I suppose I assume you're at home with your father. Why would you not be there with your father? And no, I don't bother to check with him. I don't think we have any reason at this time to feel especially worried about you.

And so I go back to my book and I finish my dinner and then I return to the hotel and I sleep. And that's all. Certainly nothing about our conversation seems to weigh very heavily on me.

And it's strange, because I still remember that restaurant and the dark street outside – the large, blazing rowan tree just outside the window, a tree so unfamiliar and striking I have to google it on my phone. And if I shut my eyes I can even see that perfectly chilled glass of wine, so welcome after all the talking and thinking and smiling –

But I can't remember anything at all about our conversation, not a single word.

Why? Why am I so keen to finish my dinner? What exactly is so interesting about my book? Don't I care at all about what's going on with you? What are you calling about? What's the matter? Why don't I just get up and go outside into the street and stand there and listen to you?

Though there are, of course, countless times in the months that follow when I do exactly that. The parties left, the films walked out of, the sobbing middle of the night calls taken because for a very long time I daren't sleep without my phone on. The freezing winter's evening when I duck out of a dinner and stand shivering in a city square without a coat and talk to you for so long and in such an overwhelmingly anxious state that

I don't realise that my muscles have seized up until the next day when I wake and cannot lift my arms.

But on that particular night, the night of the restaurant, when I am far from home and have all the time in the world and you so very clearly need me, I don't behave like a normal parent – instead I return to my book and I finish my dinner and I sleep.

What kind of a mother behaves like that?

Your father tells me not to think like this. For even if it was possible to pinpoint the precise occasion when I was at my most neglectful and come up with some kind of half-convincing answer about how it all went wrong, well, what then? What exactly would I do with it?

Rumination, he calls it.

Now that he knows its name, he tries not to do it any more. He even went and did a course for it – weeks and weeks of an evening class, to help him stay in the moment and take charge of his most frightening thoughts and put a stop to the ruminating.

Afterwards, ten minutes a day, every day, without fail.

That's all it takes, he says, with a small exasperated catch in his voice, as if this is something that should have been explained to him a long time ago.

He tells me that it wasn't that the course removed the thoughts, more that it gave him the tools to deal with them. He found it so much easier, for instance, to sleep at night once he'd completed the six-week programme.

He begs me to do the course too and I do think about

it. I even get as far as signing up. But in the end some kind of inertia comes over me and I don't do it.

Your father's very upset about this. He says he can't understand it. He can't see why I wouldn't want to try a thing that was so likely to help me. I can't see why either, not at the time anyway. Later, though, it occurs to me that it's very simple: I don't know who I am without my most unforgiving and self-lacerating thoughts.

WHEN YOU ARE TWO DAYS OLD, MY mother drives over to see us. Still in her padded, zipped-up coat smelling of the traffic and the dark outdoors, she sits herself down on the bed and she takes you from me, holding you up in the air and gazing into your face and repeating the name we've given you – saying it over and over but mispronouncing it just enough that I have to correct her, which of course does not go down well.

She says that perhaps we should have thought twice before giving you such a difficult name. She does after all know what she's talking about, having herself had to contend all her life with a name which no one has ever heard of. She's certain, she says, that it was the main reason she was bullied at boarding school.

Children can be so cruel, she says. I'm surprised you two didn't think of that.

Your father tells her, as affably as he can, that the name isn't so hard to pronounce. It's not all that unusual these days, to pick names from mythology, he says. (Mythology. How my mother's mouth tightens when he says that word.) Anyway, he adds, if her name's the worst thing she ever has to deal with, she'll have a charmed life, won't she?

My mother turns to him and she laughs brightly and tells him that he's absolutely right, of course he is. But her eyes aren't laughing, they are black and hot and I know at that moment – more keenly probably than I've ever known it – that she feels the purest kind of hatred for him and will not rest until she's beaten him soundly, made it quite clear that her power is darker and more vicious than his.

Lying you down on her lap, holding your two tiny hands in hers, she tells us that the traffic was terrible, coming over. Four lanes at a complete standstill just beyond the place where you're supposed to turn to get to our road. And then, letting go of you as you lie there with your small fists still punching the air, she tells us a story about something that happened at work that week, some misdemeanour which she had to tackle a colleague about, but which, thanks to her own sensitive handling of the situation, had a positive outcome.

Not one, but two of her superiors called her in and praised her, she says. She's hoping it will be taken into account at the salary review which is coming up.

Your father and I listen and nod and say oh, and well done and that's brilliant, trying our very best to seem interested but it's hard in that moment to care about anything beyond the warm nest of our bedroom and our newborn child.

My mother tells us that she thinks we both look very tired.

And when you're at last lifted and put back into my arms, I catch it on you, the whiff of laundry detergent and cigarette smoke that always lingers in my mother's hair and clothes. And I feel wrong to mind it, but it's as if you're tainted now, your sweet, clean lines smudged forever by the death-like odours of the outside world.

I pull you against me, nuzzling you close, doing everything I can to push my own hot smell back into you.

My mother does not stay very long that time. Your father has made soup and when he offers it, she thanks him but says she does not feel like soup, but will get herself something more substantial when she gets back home. And she hesitates as if she's about to say something else but at that moment you begin to cry. As I pull up my shirt and lift you so eagerly to my breast, her face goes slack. She stands and picks up her bag.

Well, I'll leave you to it, then, she says, as if by displaying your hunger like that, you've shown yourself to be an insufficiently attentive hostess.

The moment she's gone, your father collapses in the armchair.

He lets out a groan.

Very tired? Of course we're very bloody tired! So

why didn't she offer to help in some way? Most people, coming to see their newborn grandchild, would have rolled up their sleeves and asked what they could do.

I think about this. Would his mother – who died long before I met him – have rolled up her sleeves? Probably, given what I've heard about her, she would have done. Most people's mothers would. But not mine. Her growing up was cold and neglectful, she was never shown how to do things. No one ever taught her to expect a moment when her own daughter would enter that mysterious world of motherhood and compete with her for a place in it.

Not that I mean to compete, but I know she'll see it that way.

Or perhaps I do mean to.

For already when you latch on to suck and I feel the strong, downwards prickle of my milk and, stroking the silky, concave top of your head with my thumb, watch your small jaw moving in such a business-like way, it's true that I feel unreasonably thrilled by my own maternal powers.

A week after her visit, my mother sends us a gift to celebrate your birth. It's a large, illustrated antique children's book, one of the classics, about a chimney sweep who runs away and falls into a river and almost drowns, but is saved and begins a brand new life. Its pages are stiff and speckled with age, its muddy, swirling colour plates protected with sheets of tissue paper. In the front, in ink, in her pretty, old-fashioned handwriting, my mother has written out your full name – only one letter wrong – and your date of birth.

We thank her for this book, though rather too dismissively I now think. For she must have gone out of her way to find it and it can't have been cheap. I imagine her standing there in the dark bookshop, having spotted it in the window, and asking the bookseller to show it to her. Admiring its heavy, antiquarian binding and gazing at those colour plates and deciding it would make a perfect gift – a future heirloom – to pass on to her new granddaughter.

My mother was very keen on heirlooms.

But at the time your father and I don't get it. Thinking that a heavy old antique book seems an odd thing to give a baby, we put it on a shelf and forget all about it until many years later when it goes missing and you admit you sold it to get money for a fix.

DURING THOSE FIVE WEEKS THAT we agree to have you back at home – at our place, as you are determined to call it – you can't stop eating. Sweet things, mostly, chocolate and cakes. You wouldn't believe it to look at your skinny frame, but you can get through a family pack of doughnuts in a day.

When you aren't eating, you smoke. One roll-up after another, your small pale fingers – still so disconcertingly like the baby fingers I used to kiss – always busy making the next one. We don't like seeing you smoke, but it's something we've agreed on from the start, that you'll be allowed to do it. It's your absolute right at this precarious time in your life, you say, the only thing that keeps the pain at bay.

So we buy it for you – tobacco for our baby – even though neither of us has ever smoked, not even briefly, not once in our lives. In the shop you even have to tell me what to ask for. Standing there like a child and doing as I am told, waiting to hand the money over. I think it's the only time you ever say thank you to me, when I pass you the tobacco and the papers and, right there in the middle of the pavement, with a deftness that should not surprise me but always does, you get to work rolling a cigarette.

What would we have thought if someone had told us, years ago, when we were careful and alert new parents juggling feeds and sleeps, sterilising bottles and pureeing the freshest of organic vegetables, that one day we'd be happy – no, not happy, actually consoled – to see our child smoking a cigarette?

And yet once, a long time ago, sitting on a bus near our home, I happened to glance out of the window and there you were in your navy school duffel coat with your hefty nylon rucksack on your back, walking down the road. You were listening to music on your headphones and smiling to yourself so very happily and – this stunned me – you had a cigarette in your hand. And something about the way you held it – the nonchalance, the utter thrilling ease – told me that this was an entirely normal thing for you to do, a daily occurrence probably.

My daughter was a smoker.

It was so startlingly obvious that you knew how to do it, how to inhale, how to draw in the smoke and let it out again. And it wasn't just the cigarette, it was your face too: so completely oblivious and happy and relaxed.

You didn't even look like my daughter. I don't know who you looked like but you did not seem to be mine.

And I stared from the bus window at this carefree and smiling young girl, smoking and smiling, my daughter who did not look like my daughter, and all I felt was awe. Even though you were fifteen years old and not allowed to smoke. Even though I could have got off that bus at any moment and caught you by the shoulders and yelled at you, or done whatever it is that mothers of smoking children are supposed to do – the thing that many people, my mother included, would have said that I definitely should do.

I did not do it. I didn't do anything.

Instead I remained sitting on that bus with my face turned to the window and I continued to gaze at you in awe.

*

FRIENDS COME TO SEE US. DRIVING fifty miles or more, all so they can meet us for a few hours at a pub on the coast. It's good of them – they're old friends, good friends, we've known them for a lot of years – and it makes me slightly ashamed that I don't feel like seeing them.

Your father says that it will do me good, it will do us both good, he says, it's been far too long since we saw anyone. But I don't want to feel good – I don't want to feel any better than I do right now.

And I try to tell your father this, but he doesn't get it, I can see that. And when I sit there, searching for the words that might convince him, I catch him watching me with such a look of loss on his face that for a moment he seems like a stranger. I could almost imagine that I only just met him – a man I ran into somewhere – and for a moment the thought feels so likely that it takes my breath away.

We find our friends in the car park – it's a sunny, breezy day, bright gusting waves hitting the promenade – all of us laughing and talking as we wait for them to buy a ticket from the meter. After that we walk up the hill to admire the view. And it's clear that they're going out of their way not to mention you, skating around the subject, terrified I suppose of hurting us, of pressing on a nerve, yet always – and I have to admit I can't fault them in this, I never could fault them – with so much caring and compassion in their eyes.

It's not that they want to ignore you, I know that. They just don't know what to say to us yet. No one knows quite what to say. Many times, even we don't know.

But you can see how glad they are to see your father and me so apparently relaxed and happy, still able to laugh and still so very much together. Not that they know how close we came to falling apart, nobody knows that, but all the same you can see that this is a relief to them.

The sky's grey, then white, then blue, gusts of wind bending the wild fennel, strands of my hair sticking to my lips. And when we get to the top we all pause for breath, standing there in silence for a moment as we take it all in.

And I'm terrified they might start coming then – the real words, the ones we've all been so carefully avoiding. And sensing this, I harden myself, holding onto the low wooden fence and turning my face away.

They're not having my heart, not just yet.

Later, though, over lunch in the little pub with its wood panelling and blazing fire and photographs of long-dead fishermen on the walls, this man tells us about an incident from his past, something we've never heard before, a thing we never knew about and which makes me realise that I understand nothing.

He tells us how, as a small boy of five years old, he found his mother after she fell down the stairs. How they'd been away for the night and just got back – his father putting his key in the front door to let him in, before going back to fetch the bags from the car – and he went running and calling into the hall and there she was.

She'd been there for a while, it turned out. Her skin was grey, her head bruised, the blood pooling under her fingernails.

But her eyes were open, he remembers that.

I didn't know what death was, he says, bewilderment on his face as, under the table, his wife reaches for his hand. But I suppose I just knew that she was gone.

MY MOTHER SENDS ME AN EMAIL. SHE wants to remind me that she's been a parent for a lot longer than I have – close to fifty years in case I've forgotten – and she's been thinking about all the problems we've been having with you and how stressed we are and how much we always seem to be struggling and she wonders if the answer might be simple: perhaps we both just need to lighten up a bit?

You two are always down on her like a ton of bricks the moment she puts a foot wrong, she writes. And all because she can't seem to conform to your intellectual and high-achieving standards. Have you ever considered just taking a step back and actually listening to her?

She reminds me that I myself was a difficult teenager, moody and histrionic, full of strange, romantic whims and overblown notions. She used to worry – she can tell me this now – that I might even be mentally ill. Do I remember, for instance, how I liked to draw attention to myself by laughing out loud in my sleep? How I locked myself away in my room and spent all my time reading books and refusing to go to the tennis club disco and claiming not to be interested in boys.

And what about the awful way I dressed? Refusing to wear make-up and going barefoot in the summer and keeping my hair so short. Do I remember the time I came home from the second-hand shop with some hideous black crepe dress I'd insisted on buying?

I didn't criticise you, she says. I just kept my opinions to myself and let you get on with it. If you wanted to look like you were going to a funeral, then fair enough. That's what I mean by taking a step back. The art of being a parent is all about give and take. I'm surprised you haven't worked that one out yet.

I remember the dress. Not crepe, but taffeta – a vintage cocktail frock with a blue-black sheen like the top of a bird's head. Behind the curtain in the shop, I slipped it on and did not recognise myself: so edgy and unlikely and rebellious-looking. It was a beautiful dress. Has my mother really forgotten that, once her initial outrage had passed, she turned on the coldness and the silence, freezing me out until finally I gave in and took it back?

And I know that you're so keen on all this artistic spontaneity, she continues. But I can tell you that for we normal mortals there's a lot to be said for a routine. I wonder whether if, like the rest of us, you stuck to more of a nine to five you'd find you had more time for your daughter. Have you ever considered that your complete lack of discipline might be rubbing off on her? Perhaps if you all got out of bed at the same time every day and ate some protein for breakfast – a couple of eggs on wholemeal toast might be a start – you might find that things changed quite dramatically for you?

When your father sees this email, he does what I daren't do. He picks up the phone and, when my mother doesn't answer, he leaves her a message. He thanks her for her input which he's sure is well intended, but adds that he'd rather she didn't lecture us about a situation she can't possibly understand.

He tells her that you've just received your second caution for possession and your first for shoplifting and that, though we're doing everything we can to try and keep you at school, most days it feels like a battle we're losing. And it's a special kind of heartbreak, knowing that your child is jeopardising her whole future and her life choices in this way – there is not a single second of the day when we're not addressing it with our full energy, he says. But to compare it to your own daughter's teenage liking for vintage frocks feels frankly insulting. Meanwhile, he adds, I don't know exactly how undisciplined you think we are, but I leave the house at seven every day and your daughter is at her desk by ten. I'd love to know how you imagine we'd both earn a living if we had any difficulty getting up in the morning.

His voice is calm as he leaves the message, but I see that his hands are shaking. When he turns off the phone, he sits down and puts his head in his hands.

Late that night, my mother texts me to say that she has no idea what was in your father's message, because she wiped it without listening to it. But she wants to make it clear that she finds his anger and aggression very frightening. She'd like me to please assure her that he won't leave her any more offensive messages like that one, especially when all she did was innocently suggest we might encourage her granddaughter to eat some breakfast.

Just a couple of eggs, for Christ's sake.

And at first I think this might be it. But no, forty minutes later, a second text comes.

What I was too frightened to say to you, is that your child does not feel loved unconditionally, not by you and not by her father either. Especially not by her father. She has said as much to me on many occasions. I'd hoped not to have to spell it out for you, but you've pushed me to it now. What a terrible thing, to be unable to love your child unconditionally. I feel very sad and sorry for the two of you, but there it is.

My mother tells me this is her last word on the matter. It goes without saying that she'll leave us to our own devices now and won't attempt to give either of us any advice ever again.

When I show this text to your father, he lets out a sigh.

How long do we give her? he says.

WHEN YOU'RE JUST A FEW WEEKS old, you have to have an operation. They tell us it's a minor procedure, something that babies often have to have done. Your tear ducts are congested – it's why your eyes are always weeping and crusty and sore. Every morning we have to bathe them with warm salt water, to keep the inflammation down.

Surgery will solve all of this – by widening the ducts, simple as that, the young doctor says. He tells us that if we want we can wait and have it done when you're a bit older. But your condition's unlikely to clear up on its own, and meanwhile we only have to look at you to see how much discomfort you're in.

It really is nothing, he adds as he glances at his watch and fiddles with the lid of his pen. Just a quick local anaesthetic and that's it. Done at this age, she will never even know it happened.

He explains to us that it will be done as a day case. We'll bring you in in the morning and take you straight home that afternoon. We'll need to starve you first thing, but afterwards, once it's all over, we can feed and care for you as normal.

I ask the doctor if I can be with you during the operation. He looks at me carefully. Even though he's smiling, his eyes tell me that it has just that moment dawned on him that he is talking to a crazy person.

He puts down his pen.

Trust me, he says. It will all be over in less than an hour.

You are starving and furious and screaming when they remove you from my arms to take you to theatre. But more than an hour later, when they bring you back to me, you are dark-faced and silent.

Your silence frightens me far more than your screaming did.

Before we drive home, I sit in the back of the car and I feed you. Sitting there with the door half open, one foot on the car park gravel, listening to the birds calling in the hospital grounds, while your father strides up and down, talking to someone on his phone.

At first you won't suck, you absolutely refuse. Your mouth stays tightly closed and you stare at me as if the offer of a nipple is intended as some kind of an insult. But when you at last give in and let me nudge it into your mouth, then you latch on with a fury – sucking and sucking, gasping now and then for breath – pressing both small hands to my breast as if you dread that I might change my mind and prevent you, as if you think you'll never get enough.

The whole time you suck, your eyes remain fixed on my face. Black and furious eyes, checking and double-checking. The look you give me is one of insult and injury, of the purest, darkest mistrust – the exact same look that you give me all those years later when you shove me so hard against the double doors in the hall that my hand goes through the glass and I slice my wrist open.

YOU TELL ME THAT FOR A WHILE you let anyone do anything to your body. It doesn't matter how much it hurts or frightens you, or what the consequences are, as long as they promise to fix you up. Often, once they've done what they wanted to do with you – and these are things you would not want to describe to anyone – then they do fix you up. Because people are good like that, you say. But once or twice, even though they've sworn they'll see you right, they don't bother with their part of the deal and they let you down. And when this happens, when they trick you like this, then you lose it completely. You turn into a dangerous person, a desperate animal, someone who even you don't recognise, a person who is not entirely sane.

One of these times is when you are arrested on the dual carriageway for walking along the hard shoulder and shouting and waving or taking off your clothes and causing a public disturbance or whatever it is that you're supposed to have been doing.

You remember nothing about it later. Not even now, if you're honest, you say.

Another time, you're sitting, or maybe lying, on a bench in the park just minding your own business like any normal person and some interfering individual goes and calls an ambulance even though you never asked them to. You haven't done anything. You aren't bothering anyone. They should, in your view, just have left you alone.

They were probably just frightened, I say.

You frown at me.

But I wasn't doing anything –

They could see that you were hurt.

I wasn't hurt.

You said you were bleeding –

You make a small sound of irritation.

All right, but so what? I was just chilling there on that bench which I'm sure I had as much right to do as anyone else. Though I guess I must also have been in withdrawal and that's not pretty, in fact it can look a bit fucking dramatic. Seriously, you have no idea, you add. You haven't seen me like that.

For a moment I am silent. I have seen you like that. Your father and I have both seen it and it's not something we'll forget in a hurry, not something that any parent would. But I suspect this isn't the moment to remind you of this.

When you confide these things to me, when you tell

me about the people who've made use of your young body, when you describe to me the times you've been arrested on a public highway or found bleeding in a park without knowing anything about it, I don't turn to you with tears in my eyes and demand explanations. I don't ask you the question I long to ask – which is what terrible thing could possibly have happened to you, my child, to make you bleed like that.

Instead, partly because I am driving you to a dental appointment – but also because, honestly, I am long past any such response – I keep my calm, dry eyes on the road and I watch the green trees and dappled light and the endless stream of traffic going by and I keep my thoughts to myself.

After a while, though, I do find something to say. I tell you that I'm just so glad that you're here with me now in the car, safe and well and with your whole life ahead of you again, and also that, having seen the doctor and got your blood test results, we're now going to the dentist.

Even though it upsets me to think that your teeth – those little teeth which I once brushed so carefully with a pea-sized blob of banana-flavoured toothpaste – are so stained and brown and rotten in places. But at least – unlike all those other times when you wouldn't have anyone near you – you're letting me help you do something about it.

And because I'm your mother, the consolation this gives me is boundless, immeasurable, it is huge.

You don't reply to any of this. I guess I don't expect you to. For quite a lot of time as we drive, you don't speak at all, you're silent for the longest time. At last, though, gazing out of the window and with your small wrists resting on your knees, you let out a little sound – half a laugh, half a cry –

It is a sound that tears at my heart.

And now what? I want to say to you. And now what?

I THINK THAT ONE DAY I WILL dare to tell you everything, to let you know what kind of a person your mother really is. You'll be a grown woman, perhaps even with babies of your own, and we'll be talking intimately about boys or men or relationships or whatever it is that mothers and daughters talk about and I'll look at your darling, open face and it will go through my head that this might at last be the moment –

Taking a breath –

And lifting my head and looking at you, keeping myself steady and not letting myself miss a beat, I'll dive right in and tell you that none of it's true, that I'm not who you think I am. Not this loving and caring mother. Not reasonable, not good or kind. I'm none of those things.

I've been a very bad parent to you, I'll say, I've been selfish, neglectful. Again and again I've put myself first. I've made some very bad decisions – terrible, reckless decisions, done for all the wrong reasons. I've done dangerous, inexcusable things, the kinds of things I'd be afraid to watch another person do –

Definitely afraid to watch a mother do.

I've lied. I've been greedy. I've said yes to things I shouldn't have said yes to. I've hurt the people I love. One time – a time I can hardly let myself think about – I almost destroyed everything I care most about, all for a little bit of attention and pleasure.

Or, the words that I still find so very hard to say –

I had an affair.

His eyes are soft, frank, attentive. The way he looks at me, as if there's nothing else, as if every ordinary thing around us is closed off, hushed, shut down.

He tells me that he knows me.

He's not wrong about that, he does, he knows me. And what in this world is more irresistible than the feeling of being known? Your whole self given back to you, your younger self, your real self, with all of the wide open sunlit spaces and chances and possibilities that still lie ahead.

For a while, I escape into writing. I write a novel about a woman who lets her child drown because she takes her eyes off her at the crucial terrible moment –

Loneliness, yes, but you can't always use that as an excuse.

It is an idea that terrifies me, and because it terrifies me, it draws me in. Because I am a coward, you see, everywhere but in my imagination. In my imagination I am the biggest, most frightening daredevil, reckless, jumping into the blackness without a second thought –

Though this was before I knew what real life could do.

If this was a film or a play in the theatre, I'd find the courage to say all of this to you. And towards the middle of the second act, or perhaps two thirds of the way through the movie, we'd have the inevitable showdown. An hour of weeping and shouting and recriminations, and it would be painful, of course it would, but we might at least get to understand each other better.

And though things would, I'm sure, still be tense and unsatisfactory – real life can, after all, be so very blindingly unsatisfactory – still honest words would have been spoken, and anyway the credits would eventually roll or the curtain would fall.

AND A DAY COMES WHEN I CANNOT leave my bed. A whole, long, terrible day when I turn my face to the wall and watch the light moving over it – my eyes wet and my eyes dry, but most often wet, hours and hours passing, committing every line and curve and repetition of the wallpaper to memory just as I used to when I was a child – until finally my heart empties itself of everything and I sleep.

It eats me up, that sleep does. It swallows me whole, it is like death, that sleep.

I sleep even though – or perhaps precisely because – I know that your father is downstairs doing all of the things that have to be done. Calling in sick for the second or third time that month and looking after you, our child, answering your questions, making you breakfast and sandwiches for packed lunch, checking that you have your reading book and your pen and your plimsolls, walking you to school and bringing you back from school, making tea, helping with homework, negotiating with you about what you are and aren't allowed to watch on TV.

Now and then I hear him shouting at you and I shut my eyes to this, to the harsh sound of his voice shouting. Or perhaps it even gives me a kind of pleasure to hear him losing his temper like this, knowing that it vindicates me somehow.

Other times, though, I hear you both laughing.

Later, I'll think: this is what a broken heart feels like.

I think about how my mother left my father. Lying awake in the night and listening to the two of them shouting at each other. The plates smashed, his angry feet rushing up the stairs. The sound of him hitting her, knocking her to the floor. The bruises on her legs, the backs of her thighs. The sound of her weeping quietly in the early morning.

The time when she comes up and sleeps on the spare bed in my room and tells me she's going to take me and my brother out of this place and when I wake in the morning to the sad, messed-up back of her head, I'm confused for a moment, worrying that it's already happened and I am just dreaming that I'm back in my old room.

The time that our father gets in his car in the middle of the night and, revving up the engine, accelerates into the side of the house while my brother and I stand screaming at the landing window.

I don't know where my father goes that night, but it's lucky that he chooses not to come back in the house because if he did I don't think my mother could stop him.

Or does he come back into the house?

Months or perhaps it's years later, long after my mother has left him, I lie in my bed and listen for his heavy tread on the stairs, waiting for him to come and kiss me in that way I do not like – boozy, ashen, his face coming much too close to mine – and I imagine the life leaving my body.

And it works, for a while.

Your miserable childhood, my mother likes to say, when I take some strands of this and accidentally or perhaps deliberately weave them into something which wins a writing contest in a magazine and later, much later, grows into a novel. It's all you ever want to write about, isn't it? I suppose you think that people do not want good news and misery memoirs are more likely to sell.

When I tell my mother, truthfully, that I've never once thought of my childhood as miserable, she looks at me and she laughs.

WHEN YOU'VE BEEN GONE FOR A little over six weeks, the centre invites us to a family meeting. They tell us that they normally prefer to do this before the first month is up, but in your case, they haven't felt you were ready.

They explain that the meeting will be just you, a counsellor and us. It should last between forty-five minutes and an hour. You'll have read our impact statements – for which, by the way, they thank us, hoping they've been useful and have helped us begin the healing process. It will be at this meeting, they say, that we'll all be given the opportunity to connect and speak to each other and bring up any issues that may have arisen from our statements, or indeed anything else we might wish to discuss.

Afterwards we're very welcome to spend some time together as a family, perhaps go and sit in one of the meeting rooms or have a cup of tea or a meal at a local cafe if we prefer.

Though I do wonder, later, after we've said such a bruisingly unsatisfactory goodbye to you, whether I imagined the part about the meal. Are there really families who go off happily to eat together after these sessions?

We take the train that bright late summer morning. It's a perfect day, the sky blue and warm, the countryside golden, leaves just starting to fall. We're in good spirits and I have to keep on reminding myself that we aren't off on some fun day trip, but heading instead to an unknown town where, in a little over an hour, we'll be face to face with you.

In the time you've been gone, we've been allowed no contact with you. This is the centre's policy and we haven't questioned it. In fact, after the intense, often overwhelming period of detox – the endless policing of you, the doctor and dentist appointments, tests for various blood-borne diseases, not to mention replacing all of your stinking street clothes with new and blameless garments which carry no negative memories or associations – it's come as something of a relief.

I have to agree with your father when he says that the time since you left has gone by remarkably quickly.

The centre's in a small Georgian town house just off a leafy square. When we give the woman on reception our names, she glances up warmly, as if she knows exactly who you are. And when I see what must be your legs coming down the steep narrow stairs, I can't help it, my heart jumps. You look so exactly as you used to look – your face flushed and healthy, your limbs loose, your hair pulled off your face with an elastic. It takes me a moment to understand what else is different – you're wearing a short-sleeved T-shirt for the first time in ages, the marks on your arms almost gone. Your skin is clear, your eyes bright. It's almost disconcerting, how alive you look.

Resisting the urge to hug you, I reach out instead and place my fingers on your small shoulder, just the lightest of touches, afraid to displace a single cell of your bright and fragile new being.

We've missed you so much, I tell you.

But not that much, your father adds, unable to hide his pleasure as he looks at your face.

The counsellor, a broad and smiling man with a gap between his teeth, takes us into a room where plastic chairs – far too many for a family as small as ours – are arranged in a circle. We sit down on these chairs, spacing ourselves out rather awkwardly. I can't help noticing that you choose to be as far away from us as possible.

You sit cross-legged on your chair, back slumped, feet pulled up off the floor. With one hand you pull the band from your hair and put it around your wrist. Straightaway the curtain of hair falls, so that your face is hidden.

I realise that in the brief time since we arrived you haven't looked at us once.

Your father lets out a small sigh, a sound which tells me he's been holding his breath. Almost afraid to look at him, I reach for his hand.

And you still don't look at us. Your eyes are fixed on the floor. I long to say something to you, to catch your eye. Again and again I will you to lift your eyes, but it does not happen, you continue to sit there and nothing changes, you do not look.

The counsellor doesn't seem to notice. Thanking us both for coming, he turns to you, asking you if you have anything you want to say to us.

Your parents have travelled a long way today to see you, he says. I'm wondering what you'd like to tell them?

Still staring at the floor, you do not speak. At last, after a few moments have gone by, you lift your head and push your hair behind an ear and give the very smallest of shrugs. The counsellor does not move. He holds himself still. Looking down at the notes in front of him, he lifts a page and reads what's written underneath it, before letting it fall. Turning back to you, he asks you again what you'd like to say.

We've talked about the fact that we were going to have this meeting. And now here they are, your mum and dad. I think it would be very good if they could hear something from you.

Still you do nothing. Pulling the elastic off one wrist and holding it for a moment, frowning, before putting it onto the other wrist. I hear your father let out another long breath. Unlike me, he does not look at you, but crosses his legs and then uncrosses them, leaning back in his chair and, with his eyes on the floor, at last he folds his arms.

Unable to bear it any longer, I ask the counsellor if I can say something. But no, he lifts a hand, his eyes still intent on you, waiting. And I notice that you can't resist flicking a satisfied look at me.

You never stop talking, you told me once. You can't stop yourself, can you? It's insane, how much you seem to love the sound of your own voice. Don't you realise that everyone thinks you're a self-centred maniac?

So I do as I'm told and I stay silent. Even though there are so many things I want to say, I don't say them. Obeying the counsellor, remaining quiet. Watching as a sunbeam slants its way through the window and moves over the carpet, the chairs, turning them light, then dark, then light again.

It's lunchtime. Someone's stomach gurgles. Far away, a car alarm is going off. It goes on for a long time. At last it stops and then it starts again.

I wait.

We all wait.

IT'S NOT UNTIL MANY MONTHS later, long after you've finished at that place we sent you to – and when so many more difficult and frightening things have happened that I look back on the relative calm of that period with nostalgia – that I do a search in my emails and I find it, the impact statement I wrote back then.

It runs to five or six pages, and is a truly bizarre

document, almost unrecognisable to me now. I have no memory of writing it, it could have been written by a stranger. Some of the things that are in there, I have no memory of feeling, let alone writing. I'm not sure I'd ever believe I'd had those thoughts if it wasn't for this clearly written record of them, signed and dated and shared, apparently, with you, your father and the counsellor.

In the statement, I write about how painful it is to live with the constant possibility of your death or disappearance. Disappearance is almost worse – or so I seem to think at the time. The idea that something might happen to you and we wouldn't know. Or not know straightaway. The idea that your body might be lying in some terrible, deserted place, unknown to us, while we carry on with our lives.

I write that once, in the middle of the night, unable to sleep as was so often the case, I put my earbud in my ear and turned on the radio and it was the story of a man whose daughter, in and out of addiction and detox, accidentally overdosed. Knowing she'd done it, she called a friend and this friend begged her to go straight to her father.

But the girl told her that she could not call her father – she felt she'd used up all of her chances, she said, that she'd already put him through far too much. And so she drove herself to the car park of the community centre where, as a kid, she used to play basketball, and she crawled onto the back seat of her car and she died.

Many times, I say, your father and I have lain awake at night discussing, quite calmly and reasonably – or so it has seemed to us at the time – the very real possibility of this happening to you. We've talked about how we might find out. Would the police come and tell us and, if so, how soon? How quickly could we get to you? How would we deal with it? What exactly would happen next?

I also write – in words which must seem reasonable at the time but later strike me as somewhat self-pitying – that throughout all of this, we have both felt so very alone. No one talks to us about you any more, it's as if we never had a child. Most of our friends, even the good ones, have stopped asking after you. Or if they do ask, it's quickly, in a tone of apologetic parenthesis, as if to say they don't necessarily need an answer, or not an upsetting one anyway.

I don't blame them for this, not at all. For who wants their calm and reasonable life infected by someone else's misery? But I can almost imagine that a day will come when they'll ask me how you are and I'll tell them you've died and they'll say how sorry they are to hear that, and then they'll ask me how my work is going.

Meanwhile, I continue, how it hurts us that even certain close family members – people we thought we could count on – have turned away. One time, over lunch, when I've spent a long time listening sympathetically to the story of his wife's sister's illness, I try to tell my brother how desperately worried we are about you.

I don't tell him everything, obviously. I don't list all the things you've done and had done to you, the frightening details which fill me with shame and horror and which only we, your parents, know and can never unknow. I spare him all of that.

But I do tell this man – who after all is your uncle and has known you ever since you were a tiny, scrunch-faced thing of a few hours old – how terrified I am for you. How we both are. How living in this constant state of worry and fear feels like the very worst kind of agony, how some days it's hard to find the energy to keep on going –

And my brother does seem to listen. For a moment or two, he's quiet. Gazing down at the tablecloth, straightening up the cutlery by his plate, lining up the spoon and fork very carefully, with a troubled frown on his face. And I feel myself begin to tremble, my teeth chattering with the sheer emotion of it – the relief at having managed to speak honestly at last, because, though no one could say we were close, at the end of the day he is my brother.

I don't want or expect very much from him. I know that it's difficult, that there's probably very little he can say. It just feels good to have told him. Any kind of response will be all right.

But my brother doesn't say anything, not a word. Instead, looking down at the table for the longest moment, he at last takes a breath and changes the subject, asking me a question so completely unconnected with anything to do with you that for a moment or two I am dumb, I cannot speak.

After that day I never mention you to him again.

In the statement I add – because the centre has asked us to be as specific as possible about the daily impact of your behaviour on us – that, though in many ways our lives are still happy, still full of good things (were they? are they?), it's true that your addiction, your illness – for we do believe that it is an illness – has robbed us of certain ordinary pleasures.

We find it hard to think very far ahead or look forward to things. We've become very boring – we don't see anyone or take up invitations. We can't imagine planning a trip or booking a holiday or any of the normal things that people take for granted as pleasurable. In fact any kind of future thinking at all feels very hard to do.

I've lost my appetite, and find it hard to sleep. I don't read any more. There aren't many programmes that either of us can bear to watch on TV. Even the cinema, which used to be such a joy, seems like a pointless activity. Why would we want to pay to go and sit and watch a drama about strangers unfolding on a big screen?

Meanwhile, even the past seems to have been stolen from us. I can't look at photos of you as a baby, and lately I can't even listen to music any more. It only takes a few bars of something to reduce me to tears and I'm tired of crying, truly sick of it. I feel I've done enough of that to last me a lifetime, so I just don't have the energy for music any more.

I finish by saying that all I want – all your father and I have ever wanted – is to be able to help you somehow, to offer comfort, to do something – anything – to enable you to get better. Because if you were ill in a normal way, there'd at least be a plan. Recovery wouldn't be guaranteed and we might still be helpless, but at least we'd have the comfort of knowing that, if we followed the series of steps set out for us, we'd have done everything possible to help you.

But the tragedy of this particular illness is that the only way to help is to do nothing. Worse, actually – you're encouraged to kick your child away from you, to cut them loose, to let them feel the pain. The more extreme your child's symptoms, the more necessary it is that you harden your heart and push them away and watch them suffer.

I cannot think of a better definition of parental agony, I write, than to be forced to turn away from your own desperate child.

THE STUDENT I'VE BEEN TEACHING comes to the house. She's a rather stiff and serious young woman, thin and blonde, with severe, black-framed glasses that seem too big for her face. It might be my own fear, knowing I'm not a natural teacher – not any kind of teacher in fact – but something about the tense, disbelieving way she gazes at me through those lenses of hers makes me feel that she doesn't trust me.

I know one or two things about this girl. I know that she works in mental health. She told me that she's the person who deals with people who turn up in a hospital emergency unit threatening to harm themselves. The one time you saw a person like this – at the end of one of our most difficult and frightening days – I was just so in awe of the young woman's calm, frank energy.

Just like this girl I'm teaching, the woman you saw was young – barely ten years older than you were, probably. Her hair was streaked with pink and there was a tattoo of a bird on her wrist. Asking us, very calmly and politely, if the two of you could be left alone, she sat in that side room with you for well over an hour. When at last she came out there was a drained kind of fatigue on her face, but something about the fierce way she held herself told me she was undeterred.

Looking down at her clipboard with its various papers, tucking her pink hair behind her ear, she told us that you'd agreed to go into hospital for a couple of nights – she'd managed to convince you, she said, that it was in your best interests to do this – and she named the mental health unit which wasn't far from where we lived, just around the corner, in fact, from the place where your father sometimes played tennis.

She told us you'd be taken straight there now by ambulance, but that we could visit you the next day – she believed that visiting started at ten but she'd check this for us. She suggested we might want to bring you some home comforts – maybe an extra pillow or some biscuits or something to read. And then, perhaps because I didn't seem to have very much to say to all of this, she reached across and took hold of my arm and she squeezed it. And it wasn't until then that I understood that tears were falling down my face.

If I was being honest with this girl – if she was paying me to tell her the truth rather than to teach her how to write – I'd say, why bother trying to make up stories, when in your real life you can do a job like that, understanding and managing real people and their families with their very real crises? I'd tell her that I admire her more than I can say for being able to do that job and that in my view she should value and concentrate on her real work and forget all about the frankly solipsistic artifice which is writing a novel.

But of course I don't tell her this.

This is our second session together. And since the first didn't go so well, I go out of my way this time to put her at her ease, making tea and chatting to her about things that are nothing to do with writing while I wait for the kettle to boil.

She admires my coat which is hanging on the back of the door and I tell her where I got it and when she widens her eyes because it's an expensive shop, I quickly make it clear that it was in a sale. Less than half price, I tell her. After that, loathing my hunger for approval, I sit down with her and go over the pages she's sent me.

They aren't very promising. Not so much badly written, for she's bright and knows how to construct a plausible sentence, but just so very backbreakingly reasonable. All of her characters are pleasant, honest and self-scrutinising, all of their lives easy and calm. Not one conversation contains a single moment of controversy or tension and the one time something bad seems to be about to happen, someone else conveniently steps in and sorts it out.

We talk for a while about this crucial lack of jeopardy and discuss what steps she might take to fix it. I explain to her that the problem, in my view, is one of narrative attitude – namely that there isn't any.

I don't know why I'm being told any of this, I say. The real trouble is, I don't know what it's all for.

Does it need to be 'for' anything? she asks me.

We both look down at the pages which are laid out on the table between us.

I need to be given a reason to read on, I tell her.

She wrinkles her face politely, but you can tell from her eyes that she isn't happy. I suspect that she's rather pleased with what she's done. She secretly thinks it's pretty good and doesn't want to be told otherwise. I'm sure she's been hoping I'll congratulate her and tell her it all works perfectly.

I guess it's supposed to be a bit of a slow build, she says at last.

I put down my pen.

Slow build's OK. But I have to say I don't feel there's anything building at all.

Before she can say anything, I tell her not to worry – there are plenty of things we can do to inject some pace. I suggest she tries taking a chapter – any chapter – and moving it into the first person, to see if she can create a bit more attack and uncertainty that way.

She looks at me as if I've accused her of something.

But it's not autobiographical, she says. Not even slightly. You do realise that none of these people are supposed to be me?

I tell her it's not important whether it's autobiographical or not.

It's none of my business, I say, whether what you're writing is complete fiction or entirely based on your own real life.

She blinks at me.

All right, she says. But it isn't.

I smile.

All that matters is that it's convincing. It needs to demand to be read, to jump off the page at the reader. And the first person approach, it's really just a matter of tone. In your case it might actually be a useful way to limit your gaze, to leave things out.

Again, she doesn't look happy.

You want me to leave things out?

It doesn't always help to have such a panoramic view of things. In life it might be useful, but not in fiction. Writing a novel is often about narrowing your focus, making choices, eliminating things. And remember that you don't need to explain the whole narrative either – not to the reader, not even to yourself.

Not even to myself?

She stares at me as if I'm mad.

I laugh.

Seriously, leave yourself in the dark a bit if you can. It's not easy, but I promise you it's so much more exciting. Much of the real energy of a book often comes from the things that aren't said or entirely understood, sometimes even by the author herself.

I watch her face fall as she takes all of this in.

So – what? – you mean I should go through and change the whole thing just like that?

Not the whole thing. Just a chapter.

Yes, but change it completely?

I explain that it isn't as drastic as it sounds. She should simply view it as an experiment, an exercise. Creating a whole other document on the computer which she can easily abandon if she finds it doesn't work.

But how will I know?

How will you know what?

If it works or not? I don't see how I'm ever going to know.

I hesitate.

I think you'll be able to tell very quickly whether what you've done has injected some spark and life.

For a moment, she's silent. Taking off her big glasses and wiping them on the bottom of her T-shirt before putting them back on and picking up her biro again.

But what about plot? she asks me in a flat voice.

What about it?

Well, I don't see how I'm going to fit this new attitude or whatever you want to call it into the plot I'm writing.

Forget about plot, for the moment anyway. Plots are overrated, nothing like as necessary as everyone thinks they are. Just see where the words take you.

But, she says – and her face is growing more tense with each moment that passes – I've got this whole novel planned out, you see. You're saying I'm supposed to just forget about all of that?

I glance at the clock. The hour's almost up.

Not forget about it. Just put it aside for a while. Perhaps start with the things that you don't know rather than the things that you do.

She frowns at me. Picking up her pages and shuffling them together then starting to zip them into a clear plastic folder.

But is that what you do? Start with the things you don't know?

I laugh.

Me? I never know anything. I rarely understand a word of what I'm writing. Seriously, I always write from a place of complete darkness.

Now there's something like horror in her eyes.

And that works? You can really write like that?

Not always, no. But it's just the way I have to do it. Often I don't understand what I've written until I've finished it, sometimes not even then. But I don't think I'd ever write anything if I knew where it was going. Why start something if you already know how it ends? I worked out long ago that the only reason I write is in order to find out what I want to say.

Still clutching her folder, she sits back in her chair.

But I already know what I want to say!

And I look at her dismayed face and it occurs to me then that I might be doing something very stupid. My one task – my only task – is to make this bright and willing young woman believe she might be capable of writing a novel. If I can't convince her of that – if I succeed in putting her off – then it's entirely possible that she'll never come back to me for another session.

I push the thought away.

But imagine if you didn't, I say. If you quite literally had no idea what words were coming next – if writing a novel felt like striking out into the unknown, into a part of your deepest most hidden self, a part that even you hadn't yet managed to glimpse or properly understand –

She blinks at me.

Sounds a bit bloody scary.

Of course it's scary. But think of how exhilarating it might be.

Two

THE WAY HE COMES BACK INTO my life is simple, almost frighteningly so. One day, I find myself taking a wrong turn down some city street and suddenly there he is – the exact same person I once knew, nothing other about him, nothing different, not even really looking any older – a bright bruise opening up inside me –

After all these years, standing right here in front of me, frowning and laughing and shaking his head. And he's saying something – I don't know what it is that he's saying – can barely bring myself to look at him in fact. In all this time – or so I tell myself – I haven't thought about him once. He has even, I would say, so completely ceased to exist for me that it does not seem physically possible that he should be standing here –

This is what I tell myself.

Though just thinking these thoughts makes my cheeks grow hot.

He doesn't seem to notice. Smiling now, standing here on this cold and windy city pavement and hugging his briefcase and asking me how I am and what I've been up to.

But of course, he adds, I know what you've been up to – I probably know everything about you. My wife and I, we've read all your books.

His wife. I blush again.

For a while, when I was too young and tentative about myself to know any better, I was deeply in love with this man and, or so he said, he loved me too. He was tall and blond, wiry and clever, hard to please and unpredictable, I felt lucky to be seen and noticed by him. He never made me laugh, but laughter wasn't so important to me then. He absorbed me, excited me, lit me up. I wanted to be with him forever.

And then one day after a brief and I am sure inconsequential argument, I found myself walking up out of his basement flat and into the wide and open and sunlit street and – here's the strange bit – I just kept on walking. Continuing on to the corner, past a skip and a lorry, past the grey-faced woman smoking outside the dry-cleaner's and a man whistling as he bounded up some steps and pressed a doorbell – I kept on walking without once looking back.

And when it became clear that he wasn't going to come after me, something inside me – a brightly alive and surging thing – told me that it was OK to keep going and so on I went, through the traffic and past all the people and the buildings and, feeling the sun hot on my neck, I realised that my spirits were lifting.

It was a beautiful day. The light, it was dazzling.

And that was that. He never contacted me and I never contacted him – years and time and worlds sliding past – and we never saw each other again.

Until now.

More than twenty years have passed but he doesn't seem any different. That face, that voice, those lively, blue upsetting eyes. The shock of straight pale hair, barely even grey at the temples. He does not seem to have aged at all.

I know that I have aged.

I look at his two hands which are wrapped around the briefcase and realise with a small shiver of amazement that they're the exact same hands that I remember – slender, sturdy fingers, the creases over the knuckles still so completely familiar. Can these hands really have been out there all this time?

He's still smiling, standing there with his head on one side, looking at me.

I can't believe this, he says. Is it really you? – he shakes his head, still disbelieving – I've missed you, you know.

Don't be silly.

His face changes.

I have. I did think about writing to you, you know –

You did?

Years ago, when your first book came out. I read an interview in the paper, I can't remember where. All those times, when you insisted you were going to be a writer. You'll laugh, but when I read that you'd finally done it, I felt a little bit proud.

I do laugh and so does he. I ask him what he's doing. Is he still doing the same thing? He shrugs, glancing down at the pavement.

Same thing, different firm. And there've been a few in between, of course. I was overseas for fifteen years, went all over the place. But I've had enough. I'm planning to give it all up in a year or two.

What? – I can't help smiling – And buy a yacht and sail around the world?

He lifts his eyes.

Is that what I used to say?

You don't remember? When my mother used to interrogate you about your life plan?

I expect him to laugh, but instead his face falls.

Well, then, I guess not much has changed, has it? Though I thought perhaps I'd do it the other way round: retire early, you see, and then have my mid-life crisis.

There are worse things to do, I tell him, suddenly ashamed to have teased him about it. I ask him if he and his wife have any children.

He blinks.

Four boys, would you believe? We started late but they just kept on coming. No jokes about football teams, please. And you?

When I tell him, he nods as if it changes nothing.

And your mother, how is she?

I tell him she's OK, that she's still the same.

Still hot?

What?

I used to think your mother was hot. Come on, you know that, everyone did.

When I can't find any reply to this, he laughs again and takes a breath, still gazing at me.

We should meet up again, have a drink. It'd be good to catch up properly. I haven't any cards on me, but give me your number and I'll put it straight in my phone. Don't worry, he adds when he sees my face. I promise I'm not going to start stalking you.

But I must seem to hesitate, because he asks me what's the matter. Standing there on that busy street as the wind lifts his hair and the buses go shuddering past us –

You don't want to meet up?

I just wonder if it's a good idea, that's all –

What do you mean? Why wouldn't it be a good idea?

I don't know, I say, because I don't. It's just –

Just what?

I don't know.

And it all comes back to me then, the way he'd always

question and question me, vigorous and withholding, finding every little last weakness in the way I chose to phrase things – knowing that I'd never be able to come up with the answers or excuses that would satisfy him.

He regards me thoughtfully.

Well, I'm sorry but I can't just run into you like this after all these years and say hello and goodbye and that's that.

You can't?

No, I can't.

I try to smile, but the words are out before I can even think about them.

But I thought you hated me.

It is astonishing, how quickly his face alters.

Hate you? Why on earth would I hate you?

And I try to think of a reason why this man should hate me. Even though, in the deepest, most uncomfortable part of my mind, the place where the truest and most unsettling thoughts lie, I know very well that he despises me. That he always did.

I tell him I don't know why he would hate me.

And he smiles then, a small smile of triumph. Or perhaps it isn't triumph, but pity. Or even possibly coldness. Yes, coldness. It occurs to me that I've become very bad at reading people these last few years.

I can't believe you'd say that, that I'd hate you. Such a strong word, such utter bloody rubbish, too. Please don't ever let me hear you say that again, OK?

OK, I say, but a shiver goes through me, because here I am, after all this time, being told all over again what to think and say and feel.

He takes a breath.

Look, I have a meeting to get to, but I'm afraid I'm not leaving here until I have your number.

And so I tell it to him – the small frown on his face suddenly so very achingly familiar as he types it in. He puts the phone away, satisfied.

I'll text you, he says. He turns as if to go, but then he hesitates, smiling again. You're looking very well, you know.

So are you.

No, I mean it, I'm not just being polite. You always had a glow about you and you haven't lost it. I used to think you looked just like a painting, as if some artist had in that moment put the finishing touches to you and stepped back –

I begin to laugh, but stop when I see his face.

I'm not joking. It's what I used to think. Did I never tell you that? – his face is so serious that for a quick moment I am touched – Well, I did. I thought it. And it's definitely still there, that glow.

Thank you, I say.

You don't need to thank me, funny girl – he sighs. I envy you your writing, you know. Following your heart like that, I imagine it must feel so satisfying. More and more these days I find myself craving a new adventure.

Because it's so clear that he wants me to, I ask him what kind of an adventure.

For a moment he looks lost. But then he smiles and it's the old smile, the one that always pulled me in.

I don't know. Any adventure that's going, I suppose. Though I didn't mean it about the yacht, you know. I never did.

You didn't?

He laughs.

Silly girl. I forgot how gullible you are. That was just a joke. I don't like sailing at all, in fact if I'm honest, I can't think of anything worse.

YOU'RE ORIGINALLY SUPPOSED TO BE DETAINED in the mental health unit for at least two days, but in the end it's less than twenty-four hours. We see you into the ambulance that night and the following morning I go straight back to visit you. I go alone. Your father and I agree that both of us together might overwhelm you. You often complain that as a couple we gang up on you, as if it's abnormal – or even an outright injustice – to be the offspring of two parents, rather than one.

I take you a pillow as suggested, as well as some clean underwear, a hoodie and some chocolate. The young woman assured us they wouldn't let you go through withdrawals in there, but I don't know what they'll have given you and I know you'll be feeling rough. At the last minute, I also grab a couple of the old music magazines from the pile by your bed. I have no idea why I do this, since you haven't touched them in as long as I can remember.

The unit is only a couple of miles from our home, but I can't face walking so I take a taxi there. The driver's a big man with a copper bracelet on his wrist and a picture of a toddler dangling from his mirror. When I give him the address of the unit, he looks at me in the mirror and asks me if I work there.

When I tell him that no, I'm going to see my daughter, he shakes his head and says he's sorry to hear that and then he asks me a few more questions about you which I try to answer as honestly as I can. He apologises then, for the intrusion, saying he doesn't mean to be nosy. I tell him it's not nosy, that I don't mind at all. After a couple more minutes have passed, he checks my face in the mirror and tells me again how sorry he is.

The unit is on a large estate with high fences and long driveways and rows of parking spaces bordering each separate building. I tell him it's fine to drop me at the bottom, but he won't have it and insists on driving me up to the door. Refusing to charge me the full fare, he tells me he hopes things turn out well for you.

It's a bright and sunny Saturday morning. Outside you can hear children playing and an ice-cream van doing its rounds. But once inside the unit, time stops – the air's thick and dead, heavy with the odour of old food. Because it's the weekend, there are few staff around. Once I've been let in through the two sets of locked double doors, I'm left alone in a long corridor where, the woman on reception assures me, you'll soon be brought to me.

The corridor's airless – despite the warm weather all the radiators seem to be on. I sit there for some time but there's no sign of you – no sign of anyone in fact – though now and then I hear the far-off sound of a radio and a woman laughing. In the corridor there are many doors. I wonder if they're offices. At one point, sick of waiting, I get up and try one of the handles but am not all that surprised to find it locked.

I think briefly about going back to reception, but don't want to risk missing you if someone comes. I look at my watch. More than half an hour has passed.

Just as I'm about to give up, a different woman comes and asks me my name and then escorts me down the corridor to a kind of indoor courtyard or atrium. Sun streams in through the vaulted glass roof, lighting up the artificial grass, the plastic benches and the huge and dusty artificial plants. In this eerily bright, hot room, several men and women are sitting around in their dressing gowns and smoking cigarettes.

When I come in, they all raise their heads and gaze at me with expressionless eyes.

The woman asks me if any of these people are my

daughter. When I tell her no, you definitely aren't here, she looks flustered. She tells me that in that case it's possible you've gone out.

What? I say. You mean out of the unit?

It would look like it, yes.

But she's not allowed to go out.

Not unless a family member signs her out, the woman corrects me.

When, feeling more and more anxious, I explain that no family member could possibly have done this, she frowns at me and says we should go and take a look at the book.

The book?

In reception. To see if she's been signed out.

We return to reception. Straightaway the original woman, the one who spoke to me when I came in, says, Oh yes, I remember now, her boyfriend came a while ago. I think they popped out for something to eat.

Her boyfriend? I feel the blood drain from my body.

I tell the woman that you don't have a boyfriend. Her cheeks change colour but she does not give any ground. Peering at the signature in the book.

Tall chap, dark hair, nice looking?

Beginning to panic, I tell her I have no idea who this can be.

Well, she certainly knew him, she says.

*

THE BAR'S HIGH UP, AT THE top of the tallest building in the city. A strange kind of place, he says in his email, but trust me, the views are worth it.

It's a freezing night, the first flakes of snow just beginning to squeeze themselves out of the sky. By the time I arrive it's coming down properly, people brushing their hair and stamping their feet as they come into the vast marble foyer.

Once inside, there's a long queue for security checks. It occurs to me that I could just leave, but I don't leave. Instead I wait to go through and then get in the lift as he instructed me – thirty-eight floors, thirty-nine –

I come out to find him standing there waiting with his big coat over his arm. He is smiling but I can see that his eyes are afraid.

I didn't think you'd come, he says. I kept on checking my phone for a text.

I laugh. Because it's true that I almost changed my mind.

The place is packed, dimly lit, a piano being played. The women are in skirts, the men on their phones. We sit beside each other on low seats right up against the floor-to-ceiling window – its blackness whirling with snow – and he calls the waiter over and asks me what I want to drink. After the man has gone, he looks at me for a moment and then asks me if I'd mind moving to sit opposite him.

I do as he says and he nods.

That's better. After all these years, I need to be able to look at you.

He's come straight from work and is wearing a suit but has taken off his tie, rolled it up and put it in his pocket. I can't decide if he looks familiar or unfamiliar. Nothing about him is as I expected, but at the same time everything is.

He asks me what I'm thinking. I tell him I'm not thinking anything. His briefcase is on the floor by his feet and he reaches down to pull it closer. I ask him what's in it.

Nothing, he says. Just work.

Tell me.

Seriously, it's not interesting.

I am interested.

He laughs.

No, you're not.

For a quick moment we just look at each other. Keeping his eyes on me, he asks me if my husband knows I'm here.

Of course, I say. Why? Doesn't your wife?

He widens his eyes.

She knows I'm having a drink with an old friend. I didn't see the need to tell her any more than that.

I try to think about his wife.

What? he says when he sees my face. You think I should have told her? You think there's something to tell?

*

HE DEMANDS THAT I EXPLAIN my life to him, all of it, he says, I mustn't leave anything out. He wants to hear about every single thing that's happened to me since we last saw each other, every little detail of what I've done and thought and felt.

But you can begin by telling me why you got up and walked out of my life that day, he says as, smiling, he leans back in his seat and picks up his drink.

Blushing, I ask him if he thinks that's what happened.

What do you mean, is that what happened?

That I walked away.

His face changes.

You don't think you walked away?

I am silent for a moment, putting down my drink, my hands in my lap.

I'm sorry, I say. What I mean is, it was a long time ago. I don't remember much. I don't really know why I left.

You don't?

I lift my chin and dare myself to look at him.

No, I don't. Do you?

He takes a quick breath, looking away down the bar.

I remember feeling pretty humiliated, if that's what you mean.

Humiliated?

Things were so good between us. I thought we loved each other. I suppose I just didn't know why you'd do such a thing.

I glance at the window – snow still falling through the blackness.

I'm sorry, I say.

You're sorry?

Well – but didn't we have an argument?

He begins to laugh.

We had an argument? And that's why you left?

I shrug.

We were young – I was young.

That's not enough –

Anyway it was all over so easily. Nothing else happened, did it? I can't remember anything else about it. That was it. You never came after me –

He is silent then. For the longest time he just looks at me. When at last he speaks, his eyes have changed again and his voice is soft.

You think I should have come after you?

I don't know. Not really, no.

But you wanted me to?

I don't know.

Come on, you must know. Were you angry with me?

No. I wasn't angry. I don't think I was. But you seem quite angry now if you don't mind me saying so.

I do?

Yes. Yes, you do.

He's quiet again. But at last he smiles.

Well, this is it, isn't it? It's exactly what we used to do. It's how we used to argue, all those years ago.

Is it?

You really don't remember? So now I need you to promise me that you're not about to get up and walk away?

I smile.

I won't walk away, I say, though it's true that a part of me had been considering it.

He looks at me for a long moment and then he sighs.

Perhaps what you need to know – what I need to tell you – is that you going away like that, with no warning or explanation – well, it broke my heart.

I glance at him.

Really?

You don't believe me? Why? What are you imagining? That I didn't care about you?

I take a breath, say nothing. I don't know what I imagined.

I loved you, you know I did – he sighs. After you left, I became quite depressed, if you really want to know. I didn't know what to do with myself – the shine had gone out of everything. It wasn't just you, he adds. Things were difficult at work, I wasn't enjoying my job. I was really sick of everything, actually. In the end I gave it all up, rented out my flat and left the city and went travelling for a while. I needed to clear my head, I suppose.

I ask him where he went. He blinks.

Everywhere. Literally – all over the place. You name

it, I went there. But it didn't seem to make much difference to anything. When I returned, I went straight back into the job I'd left, but at a much higher level. It was as if all that travelling and soul-searching had achieved precisely nothing –

But surely, I say, it did achieve something – if you were promoted?

He laughs in a quick, hard way.

Sure. If that's how you want to look at it, yes, sure, of course.

How should I look at it?

He eyes me carefully.

Well. Let's see. It all depends on what you want out of life, doesn't it? – and then, as if he's just thought of something, he reaches into his jacket and pulls out his phone. You want to see my kids?

He brings up a picture of four fair-haired boys by the sea, crowded together with their arms around each other and squinting into the sun.

Holding it out to me.

Summer holiday, last year. The three big ones still look the same but the little one's changed completely. You wouldn't recognise him. A growth spurt, I suppose.

Taking the phone from him, feeling the sudden, surprising intimacy of its smooth, hot weight in my hands, I look hard at the picture.

Scroll across, he says.

I scroll. More pictures taken in the same place and

then another in what looks like a restaurant – boys laughing around a red chequered tablecloth, the littlest one with a gummy gap where his front teeth should be, holding a fan of cards up to the camera. All the time I wait for a picture of his wife, but none comes.

OK, he says, your turn.

Handing the phone back to him, I pull out my purse and from somewhere within its folded depths, I bring out a tiny photo, not a good one – just a head and shoulders cut out of a larger shot.

It's a bit out of date, I tell him, suddenly all too aware of its shortcomings.

This is all you have?

He takes it from me, holding it briefly then handing it back. Disappointment washes over me. He didn't look at it enough.

WHEN MY MOTHER DIES, BECAUSE I haven't seen or spoken to her in so long – and, also, I'm sure, because she did not want me at her funeral – I find the fact of it very hard to grasp. The idea that her breath has finally left her body, that she is, in every conceivable way, gone, that I'll never see or speak to her again – that it's all over between us, all chance of reconciliation lost irrevocably and forever – it's a difficult thing to understand.

Hard to believe that I'll never again pick up the phone and call her. Not that I want to call her – I haven't spoken to her in a long time and, though it's noticeable that she hasn't called me either, still neither of us is in any doubt about who instigated this particular silence.

For such a long time I managed to keep her at a distance. I thought this was what I wanted. I knew it was. But now that she's dead, it's as if she's found her way right back into the very centre of things. Her face is the last thing I think of before I fall asleep, the first when I wake. At night I lie rigidly awake in the bedroom darkness with my eyes on the door, waiting for something, I don't know what.

It occurs to me that I made my mother very unhappy.

I think a lot about the early morning phone call from my brother, how clear it is that he doesn't want to tell me much. His words grim and stiff, as if we barely know each other. Just doing his duty, he says.

And yet somehow, in among all those cold words of his – which I'm sure are no more or less than I deserve – I manage in my shock to disbelieve him. Perhaps he's got it wrong and it hasn't happened – or not yet anyway, or not quite the way he says it has.

For how can our mother be dead?

It would be so very like my brother to get the wrong end of the stick – even as a child, he was famous for it. It's hard to believe that she isn't about to come striding into the room as she always does, her eyes flashing and her mouth tense as she waits for me to say something she does not like –

My mother always entered every room as if it was a competition. It wasn't her fault. As a small child, she was sent away to boarding school – put on a plane at five years old, made to wash her mouth out with soap for telling fibs, lying there in her cold and lonely bed, bullied and afraid and not cared for by anyone.

When it was Christmas, she waited to be collected like all the other children, but no one came for her. She told me that she did not question this at the time – for why would she? – but it meant that she spent more than one Christmas at school, with a forlorn house mistress and a couple of older children whose parents lived on the other side of the world.

My brother is quite open about the fact that our mother died alone. He tells me this fact without any shame. He also wants me to know that he asked her, on that last day, if he should call me and she said no. Even when she knew she was dying, when she knew that it might be her last chance. Very definitely that was her answer. No.

Because what would be the point? she said.

My brother is very clear about this.

She did not think it would make any difference to anything, he tells me.

And it was the middle of the night. Two in the morning, then three. She'd had morphine for the pain, she didn't know what was happening, they were fairly sure of that. And no one had any idea how long it was going to take – even the nurses didn't know, it was impossible for anyone to know. And so, since there seemed to be no point in hanging on, everyone went home.

Though as it turned out, my brother says, he might as well have stayed. He was still in his car when the phone call came.

My mother once told me that she no longer remembered a single thing about her time at boarding school. Years and years of her childhood gone, obliterated – they were a blank to her, a loss. And no, she didn't know why they sent her – on an aeroplane, at such a young age, barely out of babyhood she was, to that strict and forbidding school in the middle of the cold grey sea – and she never asked. She didn't bother asking later either – when she was an adult and surely by then entitled to some kind of an explanation – because what would be the point?

There aren't always straightforward answers to these things, she said.

My mother chose to be buried, rather than cremated. And, though my brother seems unsure about sharing any details – he's been strictly instructed that I mustn't be told a single thing and I suppose, to be fair, this must make things quite awkward for him – he does at least, when I press him, let me know the time of the service and the burial place.

And you're not to write about any of this either, he adds, as he warns me that I will definitely be turned away should I suddenly take it into my head to try and attend the funeral.

I tell him I would not dream of writing about it. And I'm not lying, of course I'm not – not then. Why would I want to write about it? At that particular moment the idea could not be further from my mind.

But I do find it very hard to think of my mother trapped there under the earth. For a long time afterwards, I find myself checking the weather app on my phone to see how cold or wet or windy it is in the place where she lies.

Even now I do it. Today, for instance, they say there is a chance of snow there. I think of her lying down there all alone under that freezing earth and my heart breaks.

I TAKE YOU AWAY ON HOLIDAY, JUST you and me, without your father. Our rented cottage is a disappointment – much smaller than it looked in the photos, located down a lifeless road by the pier. Not very clean either. I find biscuit wrappers down the back of the sofa and hairs in the bath. When I open the back door, the handle comes off in my hand. Out in the scrubby, concrete yard, a ginger cat arches its back and spits at us.

You run around laughing, looking in cupboards and drawers. You tell me you love it. You ask if we can come here every year.

Because I'm able to give my whole self to you – no work, no one and nothing else to think about – the days pass easily. We play on the beach and paddle in the sea and eat crab sandwiches and catch tiddlers in the boating lake, carrying them home in a bucket which we leave by the back door. You want to keep them as pets, but next day I convince you to take them back. I don't think you notice, as we empty the bucket, that most stay floating on the surface of the water.

Every night once you're in bed, I call your father. We discuss whether it's worth him coming down for a night or two, but I can tell he isn't keen. Work has been crazy, he's not sure he can take the time off. And anyway he thinks he might have agreed to a meet up with the guys at the pub one night that week.

Which? I say. Is it work or the guys?

You seem to be getting on very well without me –

But I miss you.

Yeah, yeah.

But I do.

It's barely been four days.

He does not say that he'll come.

One day, walking along the sea front, we come to a hump of green grass with a bench on it. An elderly man is sitting there. He has a long beard and a walking stick and a blazer with large brass buttons on it, like a sea captain in a story book. As if he's been expecting us, he greets us with a theatrical wave and then, propping his bearded chin on his stick, he asks you what your name is. You tell him. He says it's a very pretty name.

It's not from this country, you add.

He asks you which country it's from, and when you tell him you get it a bit wrong, so I correct you. But this man isn't listening to what I say – he has no interest in me, I don't think he even bothers to glance up. He keeps his eyes on you.

You are six years old and have recently lost a front tooth and, proud of this, can't stop running your tongue over the gap. Your hair's cut short, with a cowlick that sticks up on one side. You have shoes which light up when you run.

The man asks you if you're going to have an ice cream soon and you frown at him and tell him you don't know if you are or not. You ask him what his name is and he tells you. After that you stare at him for the longest moment.

And where's your child? you say.

The man flings his arm out at the sky, at the sea where a small boat with a brown sail is just visible on the horizon.

My child is in heaven, he says. With God.

You stare at him with wide eyes, but you don't say anything else.

Later, I ask you how you knew that the man had a child.

Because of how big his hands were, you say.

*

YOU CALL TO SAY YOU URGENTLY need to see us. At first we're worried about letting you in the house – the last time you came and we refused to give you money, you pulled three dinner plates off the kitchen rack and hurled them against the wall – but you beg us so sweetly and credibly that in the end we let you in.

Just ten minutes, your father says. And you're not to go upstairs.

Something about the way you so readily agree to this – instant and submissive and entirely unquestioning – makes me feel very sad.

When we let you in, you sit calmly on the sofa in the sitting room. You don't remove your coat. I notice that your hands are scratched, your fingernails dirty. We offer you food, but you say you don't want food. A cup of tea? No, you don't want anything at all.

And it's true, you don't look as if you need anything. You look oddly sated, rosy-cheeked, satisfied. Despite the dirt and the scratches, and the feral air, your limbs are relaxed and soft, your eyes bright.

Perhaps I'm the one who's hungry.

And that's when you tell us the truth, that you just used. Sitting there on the sofa, you let us know this fact, stating it quite matter-of-factly and calmly, the way you might tell someone you'd just taken a bus or eaten a sandwich or seen a friend.

When?

About half an hour ago.

How?

You shrug.

I injected.

A quick intake of breath from your father.

Where?

What do you mean, where?

Where in your body? Where did you inject yourself?

Here – you point to your groin.

A moment of silence as we look at you and you look at us. I hadn't noticed it before but I see it now – your eyes are on fire, shining.

You want us to know that you could so easily not have told us this. You could have lied, told us you were clean. You could have insisted that you hadn't used in some time. There've been plenty of times, all in the past, you say, when you've lied about this, times when you're sure we had no idea that you were high.

But this time you didn't want to do that. Not this time. This time you wanted to level with us – to be entirely honest for once.

So yes, it's true, you're high.

Sitting so very calmly and peacefully there on the sofa, you blink at us both.

But, you add, before we can say anything, you want us to know something else. This is the very last time – the last time you'll ever do it – seriously, the very last time ever. It's something you decided a few minutes ago actually, out there in the street, just as you turned the corner to come to our house. It's very important to you, actually, that we hear you say this.

You decided this when you were high?

A small shrug.

Your father and I look at each other.

But hold on a moment, he says. So what was it that you wanted to speak to us about?

What?

You said you needed to speak to us urgently.

About this, you say. About stopping.

But you say you only decided this just before you got here.

Yes.

So when you rang us, what was that about?

You stare at us. You seem to have no answer to this. Apparently losing interest, you shrug again.

Your father takes a long hard look at you. At last, in a very deliberate way, he yawns.

OK, he says. So what's your plan, then?

My plan? – you're leaning right back on the sofa now, arms flung out lazily to the sides, fingers spread out, gazing at us in a relaxed way.

Well, you're telling us you want to stop. But how will you do that?

How will I do it?

How are you going to manage to give it up just like that?

There's no need to go at me, you say.

We're not going at you.

Yes, you are. Both of you, going at me like that. But all right, I know what you're thinking. And I guess if I was the parent of me, I'd be thinking it too.

What are we thinking? – your father's tone is harsh.

You laugh, but your face isn't laughing.

That I'm only saying it because I'm feeling OK right now and that's only because I got fixed up.

Look, I tell you. We're only trying to be realistic because we love you and we care so much about you –

I know that, you say, and for the briefest moment your lip wobbles.

Shifting on the sofa, you grab a cushion and hold it against your stomach the way you used to in the old days when we'd sit here talking to you about your school day or your exam results or what we were all going to do at the weekend. Stroking the cushion with your small, scratched and dirty hand, pulling at its frayed edges, you gaze at us.

You tell us it isn't going to be easy. Of course you know that. But the simple fact is, you're sick of living like this. You're sick of stealing things, of living from one moment to the next and not ever knowing how you're going to get fixed up, sick of all the constant fear and the worry and the pain. Suddenly it all just hurts a bit too much –

Too much for what? your father says.

Too much to be worth it – your lip wobbles

again – Seriously, I don't know what's up with you guys, why can't you just believe me? I've, like, totally had enough.

You stare dreamily at us both for a moment and then, as if you can't hold on any longer, your eyes begin to close. I look at your father – and I ask you if you need to sleep and you tell me no, you're not sleepy, you're fine, but it's clear that you're not fine, there are tears running down your cheeks now. I move over to sit beside you and I put my arms around you and you let me do it, but your father gives me a look which says don't get sucked in.

I hold you in my arms. You are very still, stiller than I've ever known you be. When at last I pull away, you do nothing, you don't move and you don't look at me.

Thank you, you whisper.

What are you thanking us for?

You smile.

I don't know.

The room is full of silence.

We love you, your father says at last.

I know, you say. I know that. Thank you.

Before you leave, we offer you food again, but you refuse, telling us again that you're not hungry. We ask if you have somewhere to sleep – though I don't know what we're expecting to do if you say you haven't. But you do have somewhere apparently and we don't ask you where this is and you don't offer to tell us either.

For once – incredibly – you do not ask for money.

I want you to know that we're glad you came and talked to us, your father tells you just before you go.

Yes, I say, we are.

And I reach out and I put my arms around you again, and again you let me do it. Standing there in the hall I pull you to me, hugging you tight against me and breathing in the dark, sour smell of your hair and clothes.

I love you, I say. I will always love you.

Remember to let us know what your plan is, your father calls as you walk off down the road.

You don't say anything, but just before you disappear around the corner, you lift your hand and give him a wave.

He sighs.

Did that just happen? he asks me as we close the front door.

And I know what he's thinking, because I'm thinking it too. For the first time in as long as I can remember, we seem to have had a real conversation with you. No threats or shouting or screaming, no plates smashed, just normal talking and listening.

I feel suddenly very unhappy.

But there won't be a plan, will there? I say.

Of course there won't.

It was so good to see her. In some ways she seemed almost like her old self.

But she was high.
I know that.
None of it means anything.
I know.

HE CALLS ME AND, LAUGHING, TELLS me he's standing in the middle of a park near his home. He just walked the dog and now he is eating an orange, but he's regretting it because it's very hard to eat an orange while talking on the phone.

And what about you? he says. Where have you been? What's been happening? I've been thinking about you, you know.

I tell him that nothing's been happening.

My life is very boring, I say.

He laughs again.

I don't believe that for one moment.

Would I lie to you?

Of course you would.

OK, I would.

We both laugh. Then I ask him what he's doing.

I told you. I'm just standing here. Standing in the sunshine on this unexpectedly warm day and wondering what to do with myself and I thought I'd call you.

OK, I say.

But is it – OK, I mean?

Yes. Of course it's OK. Why wouldn't it be?

I just wondered if you were alone, that's all.

Does that matter?

It doesn't matter.

Good.

He takes a breath.

OK, I'll be honest. I wondered if we were going to see each other again, that's all.

For a quick second, I shut my eyes.

Why wouldn't we see each other?

Come on. You know exactly why. Look, I'm doing my best to be tactful here –

At my desk, I straighten up. He's right, it's a beautiful day. Spring's still some way off, but recently the light has changed. Sun is pouring in through every window, filling the house with light.

Tactful about what?

I'm nervous. I suppose I'm testing the waters. I don't really know how honest I can be with you –

I get up from my chair and I go out into the hall and I stand there for a moment and then I come back in my study. Even though the house is empty, I shut the door.

What are you doing? he says.

I tell him I'm not doing anything.

He laughs.

I can hear you. You're walking around.

I hesitate, holding myself very still.

Look, I say. Isn't your dog getting bored?

The dog's fine – I hear him smile. You haven't changed at all, have you?

I take a breath.

I have changed –

No you haven't. You pretend to be this grown-up writer lady, but in your heart you're just exactly the same. I don't care how many books you've written. I know who you are. I've always known. Seriously, how old were you when I met you?

Seventeen, I say, before I can stop myself.

I OFTEN WONDER HOW IT WOULD be if none of this had ever happened, if things could snap straight back to how they were. You here with us in the house, behaving just like any normal teenager, stomping around and getting ice from the freezer, making a smoothie and leaving the counter in a mess, or else lying around in your room watching sitcoms on your laptop the way you used to.

I wonder how it would feel to see your rucksack in the hall again. Your canvas wallet and your headphones and your bus pass. Your socks on the floor. Your parka – always seeming to contain the shrugged-off shape of you – flung down on the bench by the door. How would it be to hear your voice calling up the stairs, demanding to know who's home, what's for supper, why isn't the Wi-Fi working, can you have some money to go to the shop?

I watch a drama on TV where a whole bus load of teenagers from the same village are killed in a sudden and tragic accident. The village grieves, the parents are inconsolable. But then, after some months have passed, something mysterious or supernatural – or anyway inexplicable – happens, and one by one, the kids return to their families.

A mother is in her kitchen and she hears someone coming down the stairs and it sounds a lot like her daughter but she knows it can't be her daughter – just the bereaved mind playing tricks, she knows that. But the next thing that happens is an oh-so-familiar hand comes round and opens the fridge door – for where else would a teenager returning from the dead go first but the fridge?

The mother cries out in shock.

A ghost staring into the fridge. Or perhaps not a ghost, a zombie? An undead person?

But the mother doesn't care about any of that, she couldn't care less, she has no desire whatsoever for explanations. All she knows is that her beloved girl was gone and lost forever and now she's back, standing right here in front of her in broad daylight, and whatever the reason is – however weird or unlikely or impossible to explain – it's a million times better than the dread black hell she's been living in.

Grabbing onto her child, sobbing with relief as she holds her and kisses her, greedy for the touch of her, the familiar warm smell and the softness, for every possible part of her, never wanting this to end, wanting only to drink her darling girl in.

You think you've lost someone forever. The loss is intolerable. It's like you are walking backwards, downwards, some days you can barely think or breathe. And then suddenly without any warning they're back.

You don't care what the deal is, you don't mind if they're alive or dead, all you want – the thing you will take at almost any price – is to be allowed to touch them again, to hold them, to feel their nearness, to pull them close.

Watching this programme, I find I can barely breathe.

WHEN MY MOTHER AND I HAVEN'T spoken for a while – when months have passed and I haven't called her or replied to any of her furious, provoking messages – I receive a package in the post. It contains several pages removed from our family album, all stuck with photographs of me as a baby.

I know these pictures – or I used to – though I can't remember when I last saw them. In some, I'm just a few weeks old, cradled in my mother's arms. In others, I'm propped up on cushions with my teddy, or sitting in a high chair, or – a little older now – dressed in rompers and riding on my rocking horse, my hair in a topknot. In the last picture, I'm about two years old – pink-cheeked from my bath, in my dressing gown, clutching a book, and underneath, my mother has written the words I apparently used to say every time I picked up a book: I'm excited!

In the short note that comes with the pages, my mother has written that she's having a clear-out and getting rid of various things she doesn't want any more. She thought I might like to have these photos.

She signs the note with a kiss.

After I've opened the envelope, I lay the pictures of my baby self out on the kitchen table and have a long look at them. I tell myself that it's a good thing, that I'm glad to have them. I have so few pictures from childhood – everything seems to have been lost or destroyed in the bitter fallout from my parents' divorce.

Once I've finished looking, I put them back in the envelope and then I go out for a walk. It's a dark day, the city drained of light. The rain has stopped but the pavements are wet. I only mean to go as far as the park, but once I get there I keep on going. Past the lake and the zoo with its plaintive jungle cries and on through the dripping rose garden and out the other side and down into the underpass where two young people are sleeping under damp cardboard, the curly tops of their heads just visible.

At last, having walked through many streets and crossed two main roads thick with traffic, I come to a large department store. It happens to be a store I once visited with my mother, but that isn't why I go in. I think I'm starting to lose energy and anyway the rain has started up again.

Years ago, when I came here with my mother for the sales, I picked her up from the station and we sat in traffic for the longest time and then I had trouble finding a parking space. I remember that she wouldn't stop talking to me as I turned down one street after another, looking for somewhere to park.

And I know I was tired and my stomach hurt – my period pains could be excruciating in those days, though this wasn't something I'd have dreamed of confiding to my mother. Also, I was dreading the day which lay ahead of us, worrying about how many hours we had to get through before I could put her back on the train. And now I couldn't even park.

This was when she told me that, in her view, I didn't look happy. Studying the side of my face as I turned down street after street searching for a space, she told me she'd been thinking it for some time, but hadn't dared bring it up. She never knew what kind of a mood I'd be in. I was so moody, so unpredictable – did I realise that? – always so quick to flare up. She was constantly terrified that I would fly off the handle at her.

You used to be such a little ray of sunshine, she said. But now you're always so anxious. I don't know what's going on with you, but if your marriage is in trouble, you can tell me about it, you know.

My marriage was fine, back then anyway. But if it hadn't been, my mother would have been the last person I'd have told. I'd learned long ago that if I let slip even the smallest, most casual critical comment about your father – a joke about something he'd said, a thing he had or hadn't done – she'd snatch it up and store it, ready to produce it as ammunition at a later date.

But she was right, I was anxious. In fact I was always anxious in her company, always checking and censoring myself, forever thinking ahead to the next moment when I might inadvertently put a foot wrong. Visits with her or to her were tense and fraught. I could not enjoy or think about or concentrate on anything else when my mother's presence was imminent. Your father used to say, only half-jokingly, that I was never so elated and in love with life as in those moments when she had just left our house.

I used to think that everyone was like this around their mothers. But no, I knew plenty of families where the women seemed genuinely to like spending time together, mothers and daughters who weren't afraid to let their guard down or exchange confidences, women who met each other's eyes with open affection and fondness and did not appear repulsed by the simple physical fact of being related.

My mother and I were not like this. Even as a child, I was tense around her, always gathering myself, always wary. I did not like it when she came too close to me – just the sound of her walking into a room could make me jump. Everything about her intimate physical self unnerved me. The pots of thick white face cream on her dressing table, the balled-up tissues and brushes and tweezers, the ripped-open tampon boxes by the toilet, her wet and naked face when she had just stepped out of the shower.

I can think of only two occasions in my life when my mother tried to comfort me. The first, when I was small and had an earache and – for the first and only time – she took me into her bed. We lived in a bungalow then, and my parents' bedroom window looked out onto the back garden with its chestnut trees and rockery and high stone wall, and all through that long and painful night, I kept my eyes on this wall, breathing in the musty, beddy smell of my parents' sheets and watching the black sky above it growing greyer and lighter. And I must have been crying a lot, because at last I felt my mother's hand reach out and rub my back, a gentle circular rubbing, so unexpected and so comforting.

After that, I slept.

The other time was years later when I happened to mention to her that I'd gone to the hospital where they'd stuck a needle in my breast in order to check that a lump I had wasn't anything to worry about. And it wasn't, which was a relief.

But when I told my mother about this, she began to cry, right there on the phone. She said it upset her terribly to think of me having to go through that, just the very thought of it made her distraught. And I was taken aback then, I did not know what to say, because I was unused to this kind of sympathy from my mother and I felt very touched to think that my biopsy had moved her like this.

Now, in the store which we visited together so long ago, someone is giving free hand massages. The girl asks me if I want one and I thank her and tell her that I don't.

Come on, it takes less than five minutes – she pats the huge, padded chair. You won't believe how relaxing it is.

I look at her.

It's absolutely free, she says.

And so I take off my coat and roll up my sleeves and remove my watch and my rings and place them on the white folded towel and sit and watch as her small, strong hands begin to knead my fingers and wrists, a surprisingly firm pressure travelling all the way up my arms and sending a quick hot pain zig-zagging into my neck and shoulders.

She chuckles and tells me there's a lot of tension there.

What do you do for a living? she says. I'm betting it's something to do with your hands.

I tell her what I do and she grins.

There you go, then. I bet that's very interesting. What sort of things do you write? Would it be anything I've heard of?

What sort of things do I write? Tears spring to my eyes.

It's OK, she says. You don't have to talk if you don't want to.

And she pats my arm and then, clasping my whole hand in hers, she threads her warm fingers through mine.

It happens a lot, she says as she takes hold of my other hand and, pulling and clasping, does the same thing to that one. You'd be surprised how emotional people feel when the tension leaves them.

AFTER MY MOTHER IS GONE, A WISE and kind friend – a person who's known us both for many years and who used to have a lot of time for my mother – tells me that I must not feel responsible for her choices. I shouldn't blame myself for the way she chose to leave things, she says. Not for the fact that she told my brother not to call me that night, certainly not for the fact that, just like my father, she left most of her money to my brother.

Don't go around thinking you could have prevented it, this person says. Don't fool yourself into thinking that anything you might have done or not done would have changed anything. Both your parents' deaths were angry deaths, intended to leave misery and chaos behind them.

Misery and chaos.

Though the friend means well and I can see the truth in this, still it hurts to hear it. I realise that I don't particularly enjoy being told these things about my mother. I think that it feels very unfair on her, as if something crucial isn't being taken into account – as if there might be a fact or a clue out there which, if only I could retrieve it, might explain everything.

In one of the photographs that my mother sent back to me, I am so small, just a tiny wisp of a newborn nestled against her shoulder. And my mother's hair is long and black and wavy and she has on a light-coloured, cotton dress and she's pressing her lips against the top of my head and her face – she's just twenty-one – is lit up with so much tenderness.

Most of the pictures she sent, I put away in the cupboard. But this particular one, the one of me so small and safe against her shoulder, I slide between the pages of a book that I keep by my bed and every so often I pull it out and look at it.

Every time I look at it, I feel that it knows something that I don't. Something, probably, that neither of us knows.

I look at it a lot that winter.

ALMOST EVERY DAY, HE CALLS OR texts me. Telling me that he's thinking about me, that I've got right under his skin, that he doesn't know why, but even though we've only seen each other twice – twice! can you believe that? he says – he misses me.

I tell him I think about him too.

You do? You do! Go on, tell me, how much do you think about me?

I'm not telling you that, I say, blushing, but I concede that it's strange, how easy it feels to talk to him and how thoroughly I seem to know him, even though we've spent half our lives apart.

And is that a good feeling, knowing me?

Yes, I say, realising as I say it that on some animal level that I will never understand, this is entirely true. As if a part of me I imagined I'd lost forever is now suddenly so vividly and unexpectedly back in view.

The sense of space and possibility is exhilarating. As if someone has suddenly opened a door in my head and told me there's a whole other room in there that I never knew about.

He says he likes that idea.

We really did love each other, didn't we? he says.

I suppose we did.

And love like that, it doesn't just go away.

He adds that he doesn't think he can go too much longer without seeing me.

But when I suggest we meet up for a drink, he tells me it's more complicated than I seem to realise.

What's complicated?

Are you for real? You really have to ask me that? I haven't lied, he continues when I don't speak. Right from the start, I've been entirely open with you. You know my situation. You know that I have a family –

I have a family too, I tell him.

Of course. Of course you do – his tone is soft, yet exasperated. You think I don't know that?

All right, I say. But I do.

I ask him if he and his wife would like to come to dinner. I hear him take a breath.

Are you serious?

Of course I'm serious. Why not? I'd like to meet her.

He makes a noise of disbelief and then he is silent for a long moment.

Can I ask you a question? Something a bit personal?

If you want.

How come you ended up with someone so much older than you?

He's only twelve years older –

Twelve years. It's a lot. Though I'm guessing your husband must be pretty youthful?

This makes me laugh.

He isn't bad for his age, I say, smiling.

I feel him listening, but he doesn't seem to be smiling.

And – well, are you guys OK? In your marriage, I mean?

What do you mean, OK?

Are you happy?

Of course we're happy.

Why of course?

I love my husband, I tell him. He's a good man. I would never want to hurt him.

But that's not the same thing, is it? As happy, I mean.

I don't know what you mean by happy, then.

You don't?

No, I don't.

I hear him sigh.

It's just – I don't know – I detect this sadness in you. As if you're holding something in all the time.

What would I be holding in?

I don't know the answer to that. I'm asking you. Are you still there? he asks me when I don't reply.

I'm still here.

I'm saying I don't think you're very happy.

Sure, I say, feeling myself begin to lose heart. Sure. Whatever.

You don't have to talk about it.

OK.

You don't want to talk about it?

Not now. No.

He takes another breath.

So look, here's the thing. Are you listening? Because I'm going to say it, whether you like it or not. The thing I've been trying to tell you –

Don't, I say.

What?

I don't want to hear it –

But you don't know what I'm going to say.

Whatever it is, I don't want to hear it. I don't even want to be having this conversation, I tell him.

There is nothing you can say to me right now that will be good.

And for a moment this does seem to stop him.

I don't want to mess up your life, sweetheart. You know I don't. Seriously, he adds. It's the last thing I want.

I don't answer him. I say nothing. Some moments go by. I think about hanging up, but I don't hang up. Instead I ask him where he is.

Right now? I'm in the office.

Really? And you can talk like this?

I hear him smile.

You think I don't have my own office? I told you, I'm the big guy. The one in charge.

I know you are. I know that.

Another silence. I look at my hands, my fingers, the white, living moons of my nails. Outside a bird is singing, a very loud bird, bright and insistent –

Hey, he says. Don't go – are you still there?

I'm here.

Can we keep on talking for a bit? I didn't mean that about being the big guy, by the way. I was joking, OK? It was a joke, obviously.

You are the big guy.

No, seriously. I don't want you thinking that. It was a joke.

OK.

It's not the kind of thing I'd say. It's not my style. I hope you realise I'm not like that?

Yes.

Yes, I am like that, or yes, you realise it?

I can't help it, I laugh. The second one.

OK, good. And I won't say anything else, nothing, I promise. You have my word, OK? Just don't go. I'm asking you nicely. Please just give me a few more minutes – because I like talking to you, you see. I can't tell you how much I like it. It's nice to hear you laugh by the way.

It is?

Yes, it is.

All right.

You have to promise not to go. You won't end the call?

I won't end it.

You won't? You won't go?

No.

He laughs softly.

You're still there?

Yes.

He gives a little sigh.

All right then. Good. That's good. Thank you. I appreciate it.

WHEN THE THREE MONTHS ARE almost up and it's nearly the end of your stay there, you call us from the centre. You tell me that you're on the payphone in reception and can't talk for long. You need to know whether, when you leave this place, you can come back and stay with us.

Is that OK? Is it going to be acceptable? And by the way, you need an answer right now.

For a moment, distracted by the surprise of hearing your voice, I don't know what to say. I tell you that I thought we'd already discussed this. Of course we expect you to come home – where else would you go?

You make a small noise of impatience. You know that, you say. Of course you do. But your counsellor has told you that you aren't to take anything for granted, that you have to ask. Everyone has to ask. So here you are, asking.

You're asking because he told you to?

Yup.

I smile. Because in that one small syllable I can hear my real daughter.

I tell you it's fine, of course it is. Your room's all ready and waiting for you, it has been ever since you left. But, I say, I'll need to talk to your father, just to work some things out. As I think we explained before, there'll have to be certain conditions.

A brief silence as you take this in.

Yeah, yeah. Obviously. I know all of that. They've been over it with us. No drink or drugs and going to regular meetings and all that. It's fine. I know. I'll do it. I'm clean and I'm gonna stay clean. You can check me as much as you want. You can frisk me, whatever.

I don't care. Anything. It's cool. I'll even do pee tests if you like.

I tell you I don't think we'll need to test you. But we'd like to think that you could maybe have some sort of a job, I say.

Not maybe – adds your father, who's moved over to stand right next to me. Absolutely bloody definitely!

I shush him away.

But you tell me not to worry. You have all this sorted, you say.

There's this guy, you see, a friend of a friend, and he's just starting up a nightclub – or a kind of nightclub anyway – and it's only about fifteen minutes on the bus from our house and he's said he'll give me part-time work to keep me going while I get myself back on my feet.

Part-time?

Well, nights, obviously.

You think it's wise to work nights?

Not sure I have much choice in the matter –

But does your counsellor think it's OK?

I hear you hesitate.

He says it's up to me, that it's cool whatever I decide to do.

He really said that?

Fuck's sake! You don't believe me? He says I should take responsibility, OK? You really think I'd lie to you? And anyway, you add, it's a job and it's above minimum wage. So that's something, isn't it? Oh my god, I can't believe this. I actually thought you'd be pleased for me.

I am pleased for you.

You don't sound very pleased.

I suppose I'd just like to know who this person is – the nightclub person – who exactly is he a friend of?

What do you mean, who exactly?

You know what I mean. Who is it that you both know in common?

You sigh.

I told you, didn't I? He's just a friend of someone I know.

Which someone?

Just a person, OK?

I THINK IT'S VERY LUCKY THAT my brother and I are both adults by the time our father kills himself. I think we had a lucky escape.

When I hear about those fathers in the news, the ones who drive their kids out to some remote spot and feed a hose of exhaust into the car, or else tip it off a bridge into a river and drown them just in order to get revenge on their wives, I think of my father and it occurs to me that, at the very most unrelenting peak of his anger, he might have been capable of these things.

When my mother falls in love with somebody else, she leaves our father in the middle of the night, taking my brother and me to a part of the city where she hopes he won't think of looking for us. The police warn her that he's very angry. I hear my mother on the phone to them, telling them that yes, he is in possession of an air rifle – though it's just for shooting rats in the barns, she says.

It's the summer holidays and our mother explains that she wants to spend some time with us before our father finds us and they have to go to court. But we can't risk being seen, and this means no trips to the shops or to ride our bikes. Our mother tells us that it's only for a week or so. She knows that we can't hide forever and no one knows how long it will be before our father comes looking for us.

In those days I worry about everything. I worry that I might eat poison by mistake or be bitten by a snake or a scorpion or go to sleep and never wake up or catch a disease that will make me choke on my own spit like our neighbour's baby did.

I worry that our father will be so angry that our mother has left him that he'll drive his car off a cliff or take the air rifle and shoot himself.

Or shoot us first, then drive us all off the cliff.

In fact what happens is, we stay in the house for about two weeks and then one night I look out of an upstairs window and suddenly there it is, his car, waiting out there silently in the dark and empty street with the lights and engine turned off.

I don't know whether what I feel is terror or relief.

The court decides that we have to go and visit our father every other weekend. Every night that we stay at our father's house – the house that was once our home but doesn't feel like anyone's home any more – he comes and sits on my bed and tells me all the bad things I ought to know about my mother, all the many terrible ways she's wronged him, all the ways he intends to get revenge.

He tells me he's thinking of selling our story to the Sunday papers. Or that he might hire a private detective to follow her and find out what she's really up to. Do we really think our new stepfather is the first man she's committed adultery with? he says.

After he's told me these things, he puts his face up close to mine and blows kisses into my ear.

Because he misses me. Because his life is difficult these days. Because you've no idea how lonely it is, to have your children taken away from you, he says.

IN THOSE DARK AND DIFFICULT DAYS after you've left the centre when we don't know where or how you are – even sometimes if you're still definitely alive – your father books us a weekend break. He says that just the fact that we don't feel able to go anywhere is enough reason to do it.

For when did the two of us last take any kind of a break?

He adds that he's already gone ahead and bought the tickets and booked the hotel. Because he knew that if he consulted me, I'd say no.

The day before we fly, there's a plane crash. A young pilot waits until he's alone in the cockpit – just a matter of minutes while his co-pilot takes a toilet break – and then he flies the plane straight into a mountain. Everybody dies.

I watch this story on the daytime news, hours and hours of it, I can't seem to leave it alone. Taking in all the reports and the updates, the endless conjecturing about mental health and suicide, about what might or might not have made the young pilot do such a horrifying thing.

After that, I continue my packing with a strangely light heart.

Next morning at the airport, everything seems exactly as it should be. People wheeling their suitcases around in a bored way, buying whisky and chocolate, sniffing at perfumes in the Duty Free. Even the security men seem to be joking and laughing with each other.

I think about the last time we saw you – I've lost track of how long but it must be more than a month – and how, when we wouldn't give you money, you described to us in some detail what you'd done in the back of someone's car in order to get yourself a fix.

He wasn't a stranger, you reassured us, but the friend of a friend. And not just once, but several times – and no, you weren't proud of it, but what else were you supposed to do? And you'd looked at us then as if we were the naivest parents in the world not to have realised what would happen if we did not give you money when you demanded it.

In my memory of this moment, you are laughing, but perhaps that's not fair. You probably weren't laughing. I don't know what you were doing. I don't think I can trust my memory these days.

At the airport, thinking about this, I sit down on a bench and feel all of the energy leave my body. I am flattened, all breath, life and thought flattened out of me. Even in this busy place with the people and the announcements and all the suitcases always on their way to somewhere, it occurs to me that I could just lie down on the floor. And at that moment the idea does seem perfectly reasonable. And then what? Perhaps after a while I would simply dissolve, I would be gone.

I tell your father I can't stop thinking about the plane crash. The screams and cries, the panicked faces, the moment of blackness before oblivion hit.

He stands and looks at me. His face is startled, helpless, kind. He is holding a coffee in each hand and a cardboard-wrapped sandwich is sticking out of his jacket pocket. I tell him I don't know what to do.

You don't need to do anything.

I have to do something.

No, darling, no, you don't.

Putting the coffees on the table in front of us, he sits down next to me and then he tears open the cellophane wrapper of his sandwich and he makes me take a bite. Pulling the centre of the sandwich away from the crust, he makes me eat at least half of it before he rewraps it and puts it back in his pocket.

He puts his arm around me. I lean against him. The jacket is new. We bought it together in a rare moment of lightness. The fabric still smells of the shop.

I can't fly, I tell him. I can't leave her, I can't just get up and leave the country when anything could be happening to her, when she could be anywhere. I can't do it –

He picks up his coffee and he holds me again.

I know that, he says.

I wait for him to say something else but he doesn't say anything. Sitting there, holding me with one hand and drinking his coffee with the other. And after a while my breathing slows and we pick ourselves up and make our way to departures and we board the plane.

HE CALLS TO TELL ME THAT a good friend of his died recently, a sudden heart attack, while up on a ladder fixing the guttering on his roof. A man with no apparent health problems, fit and well one moment, gone the next –

He pauses as if he's still trying to absorb it.

It made me want to talk to you, he says. That clarity you sometimes get when terrible things happen, things which are beyond your control? I've been trying not to think about you, but I do think about you. I don't think I'm ever going to be able to stop thinking about you. I suppose it made me realise that.

I tell him I'm sorry about his friend. I ask if he'd known him long – was he married? Did he have a family?

He lets out a sigh.

It made me think that all I want – all I need – is to be able to see your beautiful face occasionally, to meet up for a drink now and then and sit down and talk like friends.

I tell him I'd like that too.

We need each other, don't we?

Yes, I say.

Good, he says. That's settled, then.

Three days later, we meet in a pub. I'm early, but he's already waiting in the farthest, darkest corner. When I come in, he jumps up and takes hold of my face in both his hands and then, as if he did not mean to do it, quickly lets go again.

He fetches me a drink, though I see that he has barely touched his. Sitting hunched forwards in his seat, his wrists resting on his knees. I think that he looks very tired.

I'm glad you came, he says.

I smile.

Of course I was going to come.

He makes a face. Asks me how I am. I tell him I'm fine.

You didn't mind me calling, wanting to meet like that? You didn't think it was pushy?

I laugh.

You did, he says. You thought it was pushy! He smiles, gazing hard at my face. Still, I had to do it, you know. I didn't really feel I had any choice. I had to.

He reaches for my hand, taking it in both of his. When I stiffen, he looks at me carefully.

What? It's not OK? You don't like it?

I don't know, I say, because it's true, I have never been less able to understand what I'm feeling.

You're cold, he says, keeping his eyes on mine. Look at you, I can't believe how cold you are. It's been warm today, so why're your hands so freezing cold?

I tell him my hands always lose their heat when I'm afraid.

You're afraid?

Nervous, then.

You don't need to be nervous.

I know. I know I don't.

We both look down at my hand in his. He strokes his thumb over it and, briefly, my heart skitters, then something deep inside me seems to still.

Don't worry, he says. I'll let go in a moment.

You don't have to say that.

I've been thinking about this, he says. Doing this, I

mean. Ever since I last saw you, I've been wondering what it would feel like to have your hand in mine again.

And how does it feel?

He grins.

I don't think I have to tell you that. What? he says when I let out a sigh. What is it? Tell me what you're thinking?

I suppose I'm just surprised by how normal it feels, sitting here with you like this.

This seems to please him.

I've missed you so much, he says. Have you missed me? In all these years – have you at least thought about me once or twice? Please tell me you have.

I smile.

I suppose I've hoped you were doing OK, that you were happy.

And are you happy?

Me?

Now. In your life. Are you happy?

Yes, I say. I am. I'm happy.

He lets go of my hand, picking up his drink.

And your little girl – how old is she again?

Seven.

Seven – he seems to think about this – And I bet she's just exactly like you.

She's not much like me, no. I think she's a lot like her father, actually.

Something in him seems to change and he's quiet for

a moment, looking away, across to the bar. When he turns back to me, his face is heavy – so much so that I ask him if he's OK.

He shakes his head.

Honestly? No, I'm not OK.

You don't like me mentioning my husband?

He frowns.

No, he says, of course it's not that.

What, then?

I'm sorry. After all my fine words, I just don't think I can do this – he looks away again then back at me. You just don't feel it, do you? What I'm feeling.

What are you feeling?

He shakes his head.

I don't want to hurt you – I don't want to confuse you.

I'm not confused –

He smiles a sad smile.

You don't find this life confusing? Not at all?

Out on the street, we hug each other.

I could kiss you, he says. I have to admit I am just about this far from kissing you, but I'm not going to do it. Don't worry, I won't do it, I won't kiss you.

On either side of us, people are walking past. Lots of people, streaming past us on both sides. We move closer to the wall, to get out of their way.

I'll try not to call you, he says. But I'll be thinking about you. I can't help it if I think about you, can I?

I tell him I'll be thinking about him too.

He smiles, but there's pain in his eyes.

I can't say goodbye to you. I'm sorry but I'm not going to say goodbye. Just stay there, right where you are – don't move, stay just as you are – OK, now, shut your eyes.

I shut my eyes. When I open them again, he's already walking away. I keep my eyes on him, wondering if he'll turn and wave but he doesn't turn, he doesn't do anything. In another moment the tall dark shape of him has moved around the corner and is gone.

I told him I'd get a cab home, but I don't do that. Instead, having walked for longer than is necessary, I get on a bus. The bus is too warm, the upstairs windows misted up, the seats packed with young people, their arms wrapped around each other, some of them eating food from paper bags.

When I get home, the house is dark, the door double-locked, even the hall light off, the only signs of life my daughter's homework books still spread on the table, her fuzzy dressing gown flung over a chair, the smell of the supper her father cooked still hanging in the air.

I put my bag down and I lock the door but I don't turn on any lights. Instead I sit down on the bench in the hall and I let the darkness settle around me. At last, making as little noise as possible, I go up to bed.

*

ON A PANEL AT A FESTIVAL, THE chair wants to know if I think it's true that male writers tend to write novels that are products of invention, while women are far more likely to draw on their own real lives.

I don't know this man, though I've seen him on TV. Earlier, when we were introduced in the hospitality tent, he grasped my hand for only the briefest second, barely even making eye contact before turning back to the refreshment table where a group of people, mainly men, were loudly crowded around him.

But despite all of the attention, I noticed that he didn't seem entirely at ease. Standing there in his grey suit with the handkerchief just visible in the breast pocket, using the plastic tongs to help himself to the last melting cubes at the bottom of the ice bucket, I saw that his eyes kept darting around and there was sweat on his face, which he had to keep on dabbing with a paper napkin. He frequently took his phone out of his pocket and then put it back, only to remove it again just seconds later. Now and then, even as he talked and laughed, he kept on shooting glances towards the exit sign where the temporary toilets were.

Once on stage, though, all of this changes. Leaning back in his chair with his short legs crossed, one ankle resting on the other knee to reveal a bright sock, he turns into the cool, unflustered professional. He pretends to be smiling at me, but there's no mistaking the hard glint in his eye as he whips off his glasses and shakes them in the air to make a point, before replacing them again and glancing down at the notes in his lap.

This is early in my career. I'm still nervous about going on stage. In the hour before, I've been in and out of the blue-streaked chemical toilets an embarrassing number of times, inspecting my face in the sliver of mirror, applying and re-applying my lipstick in an attempt to make myself appear more serene and plausible and defined.

I've been warned that one of the subjects likely to come up might be the sexual content of my book. All of the reviews have picked up on it – surprisingly to me because, page for page, there isn't a lot of sex. But I'm under forty and married and I have a young child – exactly the same as my protagonist in other words – and this similarity seems to be enough to make journalists suspicious.

Now, as if fictional situations are well known to be contagious, this man asks me if I feel I'm taking a risk in writing so baldly and directly about a mother who seems intent on an extra-marital affair.

A risk?

Yes. Because – and of course, let's not beat about the bush because this is key – she's a mother, exactly as you are. Is it possible that in pursuing adultery so convincingly in your fiction, you're in fact expressing a real-life longing?

Because I haven't yet learned to be afraid of journalists,

I answer him honestly. I tell him that I don't know, I haven't really thought about it, but it's an interesting question. It's certainly true that part of the exhilaration of writing fiction is that you can go anywhere and do anything – and it's very tempting, sometimes, to take yourself off to places that you daren't go to in real life.

This seems to excite him.

You daren't have an extra-marital affair, but you'd like to?

One of the other people on this panel is a poet, tall and clever, with an angular, honest face and cropped hair. I first met her a couple of years ago at some book prize or other and we liked each other straightaway. Sitting in the pub afterwards, she told me she was married to a surgeon who was a couple of decades older than her, a man she'd been with since she was twenty-one and who she was still very much in love with. She told me how lucky it was that they were both in complete agreement about not wanting children.

Now she has a very small baby in tow – she was sitting feeding it in the tent just before we went on – and now her new, young husband is out there somewhere, walking up and down in the festival grounds with the pram.

And it's noticeable that this woman, the poet, doesn't seem at all afraid of our chair. I watch as her keen eyes get the measure of him, looking him up and down, her long fingers playing with the glass beads at her throat.

And when it's her turn to speak, she smiles very

brightly and sweetly and acknowledges very readily that all of her art comes from her life, because where else would it come from?

But that doesn't mean I'm not constantly making things up, she says. Weaving a fiction just because I can – creating something where previously there wasn't anything at all.

Her poems contain plenty of moments, she says – facts, people and places too – which have sprung entirely from her imagination, episodes which have never for one moment existed in her life or actually happened to her.

But this doesn't mean, she says, that every single word she writes isn't also specific and true. All of it, every line of every poem she's ever written, has arisen from her precise state of mind at the time, her experience of family, love, friendship, of loss and sorrow and the sometimes quite challenging events of her own real life.

And I can't think of anything more urgent or valid to write about than that, she adds, fixing our chair with a long, cool look as she picks up her water glass and drinks.

There's a quick burst of applause from the audience after she's finished speaking. I, too, gaze at her with admiration. Why can't I speak and think like that? Why do I always feel the need to be so apologetic and careful and uncertain? I notice that even our chair, apparently silenced by her fire and certainty, is quiet for a moment.

He shuffles through his papers, as if unsure of what his next question should be.

The event's almost over. It's hot in the tent and one or two of the men are already asleep. At the back, an usher has tied the exit flaps open to try and let in some air, and now as she opens it further, you can hear the sound of people queuing for the next event. Having finished fielding the requisite number of questions from the audience, the chair glances at his watch and, thanking us all, throws his notes on the table. Even before the applause has died down, he is already unfastening his microphone and getting up out of his seat.

The poet rolls her eyes and whispers to me that he did the exact same thing last year. We file off the stage and, as we wait in the book tent for a modest queue to form, her husband brings the baby over and she takes him from the pram, kissing him and holding his sleepy body up in the air, so we can all admire his tiny, mauve-tinged hands and feet.

I don't expect to see the chair again, but much later, as I sit reading after dinner, he comes wandering into the dimly lit hotel bar. Standing in the middle of the room for a moment and then, when no one seems to have noticed him, walking over and getting himself up onto one of the high stools at the counter. I watch as he loosens his tie and, in an awkward struggling movement, removes his jacket and lays it across his lap, revealing the dark stain of sweat across the back of his shirt.

He picks up the menu and I hear him ask the barman if they're still doing food. The answer must be no, because he examines it with a brief, disappointed look before putting it down and ordering a large glass of red wine.

He sits there at the bar for a very long time. Now and then he takes out his phone and, just as he did in the tent, looks at it before putting it away again. Every so often he lifts his head and glances around the room, as if he expects – or even hopes – that someone might come up and talk to him. But although there are still quite a few people left in the bar, no one does.

I know that I could go up to him. I could remind him who I am and thank him for our session and ask him all about himself, waiting for him to pour out his life story to me. And probably, after a couple of drinks, he'd do exactly that.

But I'm tired and don't think I owe him anything. Tilting my book to catch the faintest of faint lights coming from the bar, I go on with my reading. And at last, a little unsteadily – in fact almost knocking it over in the process – he slides down off the stool and walks out into the foyer where, rather dejectedly, he presses the button and stands waiting for the lift.

That night I dream about him. In the dream, he and I are travelling together in a horse-drawn carriage, jolting through some dark and foreign countryside – clouds and rivers and mansions flying agitatedly past us – and he keeps on laying his head in my lap and letting me stroke it.

His hair is soft as a baby's hair. His clothes are made of black silk. I think he is crying and I am trying to soothe him – this seems to be my only mission, in fact it does feel very urgent, in the dream, that I should try and calm him down.

It's very disconcerting seeing him at the breakfast buffet the next morning, helping himself to fruit juice and bacon rolls as if nothing at all has happened.

WE MAKE AN APPOINTMENT TO MEET up with you and one of your counsellors. If nothing else, it is a way of getting to see you. At this point we haven't been face to face in a long time, weeks or perhaps it is months. Now and then you do call us, but only to demand money, and when we don't give it to you, you scream and curse. You won't tell us how you are or where you are living – we're not entitled to that information, you say – you won't tell us anything. The only thing we know for certain is that you're using heavily.

They are difficult days, these days. Just getting from moment to moment is a struggle. The smallest thing – making the bed or putting on my shoes or attempting to do up a zip – can reduce me to tears. One time my computer refuses to work – freezing again and again in the middle of a sentence – and your father finds me sitting at the keyboard and sobbing as if the world is about to end.

We're both still young, your father and I – relatively young anyway – but we don't feel young. I don't think we have any idea of how young we are.

The centre's in a cul-de-sac off a hectic main road strewn with chicken bones and litter. They buzz us in and we find you there in the waiting room as arranged. We know that you come to this place every week, or perhaps, for all we know, it's more than once a week. Certainly we know that there's a number you can call at any time and they – counsellors, doctors, health workers, whoever they are – are there to offer you help. We think you're very lucky to have the support of all these people. We are lucky too, I suppose, that you have it.

Even so it has taken several phone calls to get them to agree to see us.

We sit in the waiting room on scratched metal chairs, next to a low table covered in old newspapers and ripped magazines. The room is full. Young people, old people, but none of them anything like as young as you are. Some sit in silence, others cry. One or two hassle the woman on the desk, begging for cigarettes.

Near to the entrance, a man with long grey hair bangs the wall with his fists and next to him a woman stands watching, patting him on the back now and then. Another young man lies fast asleep, perfectly balanced across three chairs, his trousers half off, his filthy pants exposed.

I see your father looking at these people and I know what he's thinking because I'm thinking it too. How on earth did we end up at this point? How did it come to this?

After a while of sitting there, you tell me that you need the toilet. You're gone for a long time and when you come back you tell me you just threw up.

Concerned, I ask you if you're OK. You recoil as if I'd hit you.

I throw up all the time, you say.

At last the counsellor calls us in. He asks if we want coffee from the machine – no thanks, we say – and then we sit there with him in that windowless fluorescent room for a little over an hour. Later I hardly remember anything of what is said, only the flat, ongoing hopelessness of the situation, the sense of ennui, of time passing. And the strikingly relaxed demeanour of the counsellor – the laidback look on his wan, bearded face that tells us this is all so very normal for him, that, despite how ill and angry you seem, it's nothing to him, he's seen it all before.

At one point, your father grows infuriated.

Is there even any point in being here? he asks as he snatches up his coat and gets to his feet. I mean, really, what exactly are we hoping to achieve?

I touch his arm. Reminding him that we are the

ones who asked for the meeting. I have no idea what the counsellor says.

He has a gold earring, the counsellor does. Now and then he fiddles with it, moving it around in his ear. A half-eaten sandwich is next to him on the desk, various pieces of the filling falling out of it. Cress scattering itself across his lined notepad.

He crosses his legs, one hairy ankle resting on his knee. The bottom of his trainers has an orange logo, repeated over and over. It's hard not to stare at this logo as, sitting there and smiling and sipping his coffee, this man tells you that your future – indeed your whole life – is in your own hands.

Statement of the bleeding obvious, your father mutters.

The counsellor blinks at him, his face still placid.

Seriously, mate – he continues to play with his earring, turning it around and around. I'm not saying anything we don't all of us know, no one's saying that. All I'm saying is, it's up to her now, isn't it?

It certainly is up to her –

Your father sits forwards in his chair, pushing his head towards you, willing you to look at him.

Are you even listening? he asks you. Are you? Do you hear this man? He's trying to help you, do you understand that? Have you listened to a single word he's said?

He speaks far more loudly and harshly than he needs to and I feel very sorry for him then, because I know he must be feeling very frightened, to want to speak to you like that.

But still you say nothing. As usual when we sit with people whose job it is to put so much energy and time into trying to help you, you don't say a word.

And I force myself to look at you then. I look at this young person who is apparently our daughter, sitting there with her skinny arms folded and her legs stretched out in front of her, her shoes flecked all over with something which I now realise must be vomit, and I can't see anything there to love or even to like.

And this thought is so unbearable to me that I have to turn away.

HE CALLS ME AT TEN AT night. Fortunately my husband is out, my daughter asleep in bed. I flush and reach out to mute the TV, wondering where he can be, that he can call me so very freely.

I'm in a field, he says a little too loudly. I'm standing in a field in the fucking middle of nowhere and I'm looking at all of the beautiful stars and I'm thinking about you.

I ask him if he's drunk.

What are you saying? Of course I'm not drunk. Why would I be drunk? You think I have to be drunk to think about you?

I ask him where the field is.

He laughs.

I don't know. No idea. Somewhere in the middle of nowhere. I had to get away for a while, so I just got in the car and I drove – I'm sorry, he says when I don't say anything. I just had to hear your voice, that's all. I'll go in a minute.

You don't have to go.

All the same, I will.

I ask him where his wife is. I feel him hesitate. He knows I don't usually ask about his wife.

I don't know. At home. Watching TV probably. Why?

No reason.

You want me to tell you more?

Only if you want to.

For a long moment, he says nothing. When he speaks, his voice is quieter.

I want to see you. I need to see you. Can you come here right now?

What? I say, laughing. You want me to get in the car and drive to some random field in the middle of nowhere?

Yes. Yes, I wish you would. Some people would do it, you know.

I laugh. And then I tell him I can't talk any longer because my husband will be home soon.

Why? Where's he been?

At a meeting.

In the evening?

He works very hard. What, did you think he was sitting here, listening to me talk to you?

I don't know what I thought.

Look, I say, suddenly annoyed with him. You don't know anything about my life.

He hesitates.

You're right, he says. I don't.

A few moments go past while we both think about this.

Meet me, he says. Two weeks from now. In the same place where we ran into each other that day.

The same place?

You'll meet me?

OK, I say.

You remember where it is?

I think so, I say, though of course I absolutely do.

WHEN MY MOTHER IS FIFTEEN AND her father forces her to leave school, she goes to work for a dentist. And one day she's in the surgery with him and a lump of the soft, pink wax which they use for taking dental impressions picks itself up and throws itself across the room and hits the opposite wall.

The dentist asks her what on earth she thinks she's doing.

The following day she is down in the darkroom developing dental plates when she hears the sound of a bird – half cockerel, half naughty child – crowing in her ear. She runs up out of the room screaming, and the dentist – losing patience now – tells her she needn't come to work the next day.

My mother tells me that she believes that what she experienced at the dental surgery was a poltergeist. Though, according to someone else who worked there, it all settled down once she'd left.

The other thing she tells me is that in those days after he forces her to leave school, her father makes her kiss him on the lips every morning after breakfast – every morning without fail, gripping the back of her head with his large and meaty hand while he places his moistened lips on hers.

Another thing he likes to do is dip a teaspoon in his scalding hot tea and hold it against her thigh. He used to enjoy making me jump, she says.

My mother is fifteen years old. She's been at boarding school ever since she was five years old and she has no friends in her home town and although she walks around the place with a scornful and confident air – blasé, her mother likes to call it – she knows nothing about anything.

She thinks that kissing can make you pregnant. When she gets her period, she assumes she's bleeding to death. Her father tells her he would rather see her dead and buried ten feet under the earth than pregnant.

She sees no reason to doubt him about this.

And he continues to kiss her.

My mother only takes the job with the dentist in order to get away from her father. When that falls through, she marries my father for much the same reason.

THAT LAST SUMMER THAT MY mother is alive, I get up one morning as usual, leaving my nightshirt on the bed. An hour later I find it draped over the bannister at the foot of the stairs in the hall. Your father's away at a conference. No one else is in the house. I cannot think of any possible set of circumstances which would account for my nightshirt making its way to the hall.

When I tell your father, he laughs.

Well, it's obvious, isn't it. You picked it up and went downstairs and dropped it there without realising.

I don't argue with him, but I know this isn't possible. I'm a person who plans everything, a person who checks and double-checks – a habit carried over from childhood, when it was often the only way to keep myself safe and level and calm.

I never do anything without realising.

That same afternoon, heating some soup in the kitchen, I hear a loud crash upstairs and I go up to the bathroom where I find that the lump of old stone which we use as a doorstop has been flung across the room and is over by the shower.

For a moment I just stand and watch it, my heart

racing. Then I pick it up and put it back by the door. This time I don't call your father.

But, later that same evening, I go upstairs and turn on the landing light and there's a vicious pop and the whole house is plunged into darkness. This time I scream.

It's just the fuse, your father says when I call him. Come on, you know it sometimes does that when a bulb goes.

Even though he's out at dinner, he stays on the phone with me while I go down the steps into the cellar. Here among the crates and forgotten garden tools and old suitcases, concentrating hard on not glancing into the blackness around me, I flick the switch. The house beeps back into life and I run upstairs.

This is not a ghost story. But I know that my mother isn't well at this time. I also know that I should probably phone her, but I will not phone her. When I think about phoning her, something always stops me. I don't know what it is that stops me –

Or perhaps I do.

The emails she sends me are short, angry, a little bit frightening. As if she is trying every possible thing to get my attention. Occasionally I reply to them but most times I don't. Sometimes I tell myself that it's better to say nothing at all than to say something – especially put in writing in an email – that I might later regret.

Though I know, of course I do, that silence is also a tool.

My mother tells me that she's ill, that she's having

tests. She tells me that she's very well aware that I don't need her or indeed anything she has to offer. She came to terms with this fact, she says, a long time ago. She refuses to be hurt by it any more.

She tells me that she herself worshipped her own mother. And her father, come to that. Wonderful people, they were, people who couldn't do enough for her. Those were the days when it was considered normal to respect and appreciate your parents.

And by the way, she says, she's rewriting her will.

In a separate email, she lists for me all my worst qualities, all the bad things I ought to know about myself. She's often wondered, she says, what mistakes she made in my upbringing to turn me into such a difficult and hard-hearted person. So tense and anxious, so miserable and unreliable. Bad parenting has a lot to answer for, she says, as you yourself should know from your experiences with your own child.

She tells me that she's been thinking about it a great deal actually – she has a lot of time to think these days – and she wants me to know that she takes complete responsibility for the person I've turned out to be.

I was very young when I had you, she says. Very lonely and ignorant. No one ever taught me anything. I did not know how to be a mother and I was very unhappy with your father and I hadn't a clue what to do about any of it. If someone back then had offered me an abortion, I am sure I would have said yes.

She says that she wants me to know that she never reads any of my emails, not a single one. She does not feel strong enough to read them – she's noticed that they always strike fear into her heart and she has decided that from now on she wants to live a happy and peaceful life without fear or anger.

Life is very short, she says, in case you hadn't noticed.

She says that she refuses to placate me any longer. It does no good and it only causes her more pain and anguish.

She writes and tells me that her tests are back, that the doctor doesn't think it's anything, but even if it was, she would not want me worrying about her and she certainly would not want me to bother to attend her funeral, not if I have other things to do.

She knows that I am very busy with my writing.

An artist's life is a selfish one, she understands that.

She tells me that she went into her local bookshop just the other day and she did not ask them whether they had my new book as she did not want to draw attention to herself.

Some people prefer to live quietly, she says. It's taken me a long time to get the hang of it, but I have at last learned to do it, to live quietly.

She adds that life is good, that she's feeling very energetic and happy, that she wishes I could see her garden because it's looking very good –

I do actually reply to this email, the one about her

garden. I try telling her about my own garden – the seeds I've sown, the shrubs I've planted. I tell her how much I love it, my garden. We've always had this in common, I say. I tell her I would love to see a picture of her garden if she can manage to send one.

She does not reply. In fact some weeks pass, and I have to admit that the silence is a relief. Then – in a brief, accusing email – my brother asks if I realise how ill she is.

I do nothing. I say nothing.

At last, unable to sleep, I email to ask her how she is.

She replies immediately. She says that I have broken her heart.

HE IS STANDING ON THE EXACT SAME STREET corner where I ran into him a few months ago. Everything the same except for the sky, bluer, the air warmer, my heart a little more jittery and guilty and uncertain. I see straightaway that he's not quite as I've been imagining. His face is stern and frowny and he's had a haircut and it's too short. His shoes too, they're all wrong, in fact he doesn't look like someone I'd know. This is reassuring. Good, I think, there's no way I can feel anything for this man.

I don't know what he thinks about me.

I tell him I'm sorry I'm late.

You're not late, he says, adding that he only just got here. I couldn't remember what time we said, he says, even though we both know that this is a lie.

When he tells me that he only has an hour, a feeling of relief drops through me.

We look at each other.

We need to find somewhere quiet, he says.

It isn't hard – it's a warm evening and most people are outside. We end up in a dark basement cocktail bar, a place so empty that the girl behind the bar can hear every word we say. As she brings our drinks over, I tell him this was a bad idea.

What? You mean this place?

No, everything.

You're wishing you hadn't come?

I look at my drink, removing the straw and placing it on the table.

I don't know. Are you?

He looks down at the table. Under his too short hair-cut, his face is grave, the face of a six-year-old boy. A small muscle under his eye keeps twitching. He sighs and picks up his drink.

I don't wish I hadn't come, no.

We look at each other. He smiles.

Your eyes are a different colour every time I see you, he says.

When I begin to cry, he puts down his glass. Telling me how very sorry he is.

Why? – I am digging in my bag for a tissue. Don't be stupid. What are you sorry for?

He puts his hands to his face, rubs his eyes. Still in

his strange jacket, sitting there on the cramped little sofa, elbows on his knees. He looks very tired and despondent.

For all of this. For everything. For causing you pain, I suppose.

You're not causing me pain, I tell him.

I am.

No, it's me. I'm upsetting you. Well, be honest, I am, aren't I?

I look at him. He is gazing at me with soft eyes.

I'm fine, he says.

And then, before I can say anything else, he moves to sit beside me and he puts an arm around me, pulling me against him, pressing his mouth against my cheek, holding his lips there for a long moment. I feel him breathing against me. And I breathe too, drinking in the long-ago scent of him. I feel my bones start to soften. For a moment, as he holds me, everything seems possible.

Time passes and I feel myself relax. Both of us, we relax.

He kisses the side of my head again.

There. Isn't that better, he says at last.

WHEN YOU COME BACK HOME to us, you don't want to talk very much – not about your time at the centre, not about the future, not about anything. I think you eat supper with us only once or twice – pushing the food around your plate as if it's some awful problem we're demanding that you solve. You won't chat or laugh or sit and watch TV with us. You're out most nights, working at the club.

You always get home very late. I leave out a plate of whatever we've had for supper and you microwave it and take it up to eat in bed. It does get us down that the dirty dishes pile up on the floor of your room just like in the old days, but as your father says – wisely, I'm sure – there are only so many battles it's worth fighting.

Though we do both agree that it would be good if you could get up earlier and pull your weight in the kitchen a bit. Just having you empty the dishwasher now and then would be a start.

We hope that this apparent lack of energy – for whenever we ask you to do anything at all, you claim extreme fatigue – doesn't mean you're depressed. But then again, if that was the case, would you really manage to go out and work every night at the club?

Then one night you don't come home. We don't find this out until the morning and, hoping it's a one-off, we decide not to say anything. A few nights later, though, it happens again. This time you don't appear until late in the afternoon.

You tell us that you lost your Oyster card and had to stay at a friend's place. Your father asks you which friend.

No one, you say. It doesn't matter.

Even so, I'd like to know.

I watch your eyes moving coldly over him as he stands there leaning so very calmly and reasonably against the kitchen counter.

No one you know.

We ask if you stayed with your friend who lives near the school, the man who signed you out of the mental health unit that time which now feels so long ago, the man whom you know we loathe and who – though it's noticeable that he stays well clear of us – we are certain you still see.

You throw us a sour look, but say nothing.

So it was him, then –

You shrug. And a quick, dark feeling goes through me because I can't think of any reason why, if you stayed overnight with this friend, you can't just tell us.

Your father looks at you.

OK, so where's your Oyster, then?

Don't know.

You don't know? So what are you going to do?

I don't know.

What do you mean, you don't know?

I'll have to find it, won't I.

And perhaps you do find it, because you come home as usual the next two nights. But you seem more sullen than ever – something about the way you hold yourself, it's all wrong – and when we try to talk to you, you lock your bedroom door. More worryingly, there's a fresh, livid bruise on your wrist. But when I try to ask you about it – what happened? did someone hurt you? – you shove me roughly away and tell me to fuck off.

This isn't acceptable.

We tell you we need to talk. In fact, we say, we've been on the verge of having a talk with you for some time now. We sit you down and ask you what's wrong. We also remind you that you said you'd go to meetings at least three times a week but, since the second week, we aren't sure you've been to a single one.

To our surprise, you begin to sob, your small chest heaving and shuddering as if we've accused you of something terrible. You swear to us that you've been to at least one meeting a week. Ever since you came back – of course you have, just as you promised.

Why would you lie to us about something as crucial as that? It's fucking ridiculous. Can we never treat you like a normal human being and just trust you? And anyway, the meetings are your own business, aren't they? Do you really have to tell us in detail about every single one?

Your father and I look at each other. We tell you that we want more than anything to believe you. And this could not be more true. We do want this.

So what else do you want from me? you cry, apparently more furious than upset now. You want to stamp my passport? Go back to how it was when I was detoxing? Escort me everywhere like some fucking brainless prison inmate, check me in and out?

You begin to sob again. Weeping so much now that the thick black lines around your eyes start to run down your face. I hand you a piece of kitchen towel but you don't use it. Sitting there and holding it bunched in your hand as the tears keep on coming.

And when this happens, we don't know what to say. We never intended to upset you quite so much and we tell you this. We tell you how sorry we are, how much we love you, and how proud we both are of how very well you've been doing.

You're clean, I say as I reach over for a hug and, when you don't respond, make do with stroking your skinny arm.

Don't think for one moment that we underestimate what an achievement that is, your father tells you.

You stop crying.

OK, you say. You'll go to meetings, three times a week, you promise, without fail. If that's what it's going to take to convince us, then it's a no-brainer, you'll do it, of course you will.

We both smile at you.

And you do, it's true, go to a meeting that evening. We know this because we're told, much later, that someone saw you there. But you don't come home afterwards, in fact you don't come home at all that night and not the next night either. Days pass and you still don't come back. Four days we wait, five. When we call your mobile it goes straight to voicemail.

Parents of any ordinary teenager would call the police. But we don't call the police. Instead we stand there together in the hall – scene of so many bloody battles and crimes – and we just look at each other.

So that's that, your father says, because he knows as well as I do what this means.

And when he understands what he's just said, the air seems to go out of him. He sits down exactly where he is on the bottom step of the stairs and he puts his head in his hands and he sobs.

A week later, you are back on the streets. And a week after that, even though we've changed the locks, you manage to get into our house through the one window in the basement which has never locked properly, and steal seventy pounds from my purse. You also take a yoghurt from the fridge and, though we'd never have known if you hadn't made a point of telling us later, several spoons and some foil from the kitchen drawer.

We console ourselves with the fact that at least you waited until you were out of the house before stealing from us. You at least respected us enough not to take anything while you were living at home, not as far as we know anyway.

I think this is the first relapse – I'm fairly sure it is. Though whenever your father and I try to put an order on these things, we seem to lose all grip on chronology.

Three

WHEN YOU'RE STILL SMALL ENOUGH that we aren't yet tied to school holidays and, for a month or two, your father is between jobs, we rent an apartment in a foreign city for the summer. Picking up our lives and – simply because we can – living them somewhere else for a while.

In the mornings I do my work, while he takes you to the playground. Then we all eat lunch under the awning on the terrace with its view of the slow green river. In the afternoons we put you down for a nap, leaving you on your bed with some toys and books and crayons. Sometimes you just play and sing to yourself but if we're lucky you fall asleep – and then we make love very quietly, careful to smother our cries, keeping the door open just a crack, so we'll hear you if you call out.

It does feel very exciting, stealing pleasure in this way. The enforced silence, the hum of the air conditioning, the eerie emptiness of the terrace outside – and your father, suddenly and tantalisingly unfamiliar to me, with his warm thighs and rough, eager tongue and the scent of lunchtime tomatoes and wine and the heat of the city still on him.

Sometimes, if we let you sleep too long – for it's very tempting to doze off on those cool sheets afterwards – you wake up grumpy and red-cheeked, your hair stuck sweatily to your face. And this isn't good – it means you won't sleep so well that night – and then we're annoyed with ourselves for letting it happen.

Though later I look back on this with astonishment: is it really possible that we ever worried about such things?

In the evenings, as the air cools and the pavements are drowned in shadow, we walk to a trattoria, all three of us holding hands, laughing and singing, your father and I swinging you along between us. We play the game of counting cats, sometimes dogs. One time, I think we even count nuns.

But one night, moving through those streets at dusk, we find an old lady. Her clothes are ragged, her shoes just pieces of cloth held together with tape, and she's bent over almost double and, with what look like a pair of tweezers, is picking up cigarette butts from between the ancient paving stones. For a while we all stand in silence, watching as she pinches each one up with her tweezers before making her slow way over to a low wall and laying it down.

I don't know how long she's been working, but already the wall is covered in piles and piles of these butts. Though at any moment – as your father points out – someone could come along and knock them all off. Just one careless sweep of an arm, that's all it would take –

I don't know what happens next. Probably your father lifts you up onto his shoulders and we continue on to the little place with the red checked tablecloths and the blackboard outside, where the waiters will make such a fuss of you, bringing you breadsticks and peach juice and an extra cushion for the chair. We eat dinner and then we go back to the apartment and we put you to bed.

But now when I think back to that rare summer, it's not you or your father I think about. I don't think about the good times we had – the museums full of hush and history, the market with its piles of cherries and apricots, the little playground where we spent so many hours or that baking hot terrace with its views over the river. I don't even think about that cool and shady bedroom where – in a time that now feels so unlikely that it breaks my heart – we so lazily and silently took our pleasure while you slept.

No, all I can see is the old lady. She comes to me again and again – in my imagination and also in my dreams – bent over almost double on that hot dark street, always intent on her seemingly endless task.

NOTHING HAS REALLY CHANGED BETWEEN us, the only thing that has changed is we don't try not to meet. We don't talk about it, we don't say we can or we can't or we should or we shouldn't – we don't make excuses for the terrible thing we are doing, we don't even let ourselves think too hard about it any more, we just do it.

It isn't very hard, once we let ourselves start.

In fact it's shockingly easy.

One night in summer, the middle of the long hot summer that seems to be going on forever, we're standing pressed up against each other in the shadows of some street or other, his hands on my face, inside me, inside my clothes. My edges blurred with kissing, everything about me blurred and kissed and raw. After a moment, he pulls his face away, pushing my hair from my cheek.

We can't ever sleep together, he says. You do know that, don't you?

I look at his face, his mouth.

I don't know if I know it or not. All I know is that the simple ordinary things that used to give me so much unforced pleasure – walking down a sunny street, parking the car, pushing a supermarket trolley, talking to my husband, my daughter, my friends, laughing, working, thinking, writing – they're gone, they don't exist any more.

These days I am alone, always, moving slowly along the bottom of a deep, deep ocean of loneliness, living only for the moments when I can surface to meet him, see him, find him, talk to him, touch him.

Who would have thought that love could be so lonely?

Now the pubs are closing, people coming out, noise. A car backs into the street we're standing in, covering us for a moment with its full, bright beam, before then moving away again.

He shields me from it, pushing me back against the wall.

Don't you want to know why? he says.

The street's dark again. His eyes are dark. I can smell the sharp, tired, smell of his day in the office. He places his two hands on the wall and he looks at me.

It's because I'm helpless around you, don't you see that? Because if I slept with you, if I actually let myself do it, then that would be it. I'd love you too much. I'd never be able to go back to my family, never, it just wouldn't be possible. And then, well, my life would be over.

Over?

His face is soft. He reaches to lift my hair and place it over my shoulder.

Well, think about it. I'd lose everything.

For a quick, terrible moment I just look at him. My throat growing cold, my heart, every bit of me growing cold. I shut my eyes and then I open them again.

I should just walk away, I say.

What?

Right now. Listening to you say these things. I should just walk away –

He stares at me as if he still doesn't understand.

Listen to what you're saying, I tell him. Can't you hear yourself? Your life would be over? You think I can be with you when you're happy to say these things, to push me away like that?

For perhaps the first time ever, I pull myself from his arms. He stares at me and I see that his face is ragged, distraught, tears are standing in his eyes.

You really think that's what I'm doing? Pushing you away? Do you?

I say nothing, then I tell him that yes, yes, it is what I think – and after that I begin to cry. He reaches for me, holding out his hand to me, for me, folding me to him. At first I don't want to let him do it, but then I do, I find myself letting him do it. He strokes my head, lets out a small sigh. When he speaks his voice is cracking.

You don't get it, do you? It's the exact opposite – nothing could be further from the truth. I'm trying to tell you that I can't trust myself around you. I'm not pushing you away, my darling, can't you see, I'm pulling you close?

A week later, though, he texts to tell me it isn't worth

meeting up because he only has half an hour. Less than half an hour because he has a meeting and it is bound to go on longer and after that he has to go to the opera with his wife and he can't be late because they are meeting two other couples in the crush bar at six.

Couples. Crush bar. Wife.

Pushing the words from my mind.

I tell him that I don't care, that half an hour is worth it to me. And I tell my husband that I'm going out for a walk – lying to him in the way that comes so blisteringly naturally these days – and then I take two trains across the city, all so that I can stand beside some bins in a damp yard between two buildings in a neighbourhood I will never visit again, and be pressed hard against this man and held in his arms.

Another day I am ill, my throat swollen and my head bursting with pain. I think I am running a fever. He tells me I shouldn't have come, that I should be at home in bed, wrapped up and comfortable.

He's right. But. Home. Bed. Oh no.

I lean my head back against the banquette and the waiter brings me a glass of water. I drop in the pills, watch them fizz and dissolve, hurting my throat as they slide down. My eyes ache. I close them. Reaching for his strong cool hand. I ask him to talk to me.

You're not well enough to talk.

No, you – you do the talking.

He is silent. Looking down at the table.

Please, I beg him. Just say something –

His face is tense. He is stroking my fingers.

I never know what to say to you, he says at last.

And in a single, terrible moment of feverish clarity, I see that this is true. We never say anything real to each other, we have nothing to say –

We are nothing to each other. Nothing real connects us.

All we ever talk about is love.

And so he puts me into a cab and I go home and I get into bed and my husband brings me soup and he does talk to me, telling me about his day at the office and keeping me entertained, not expecting me to say anything back, gathering up the plates, the cups.

You'll be better in the morning, he says.

Letting my eyes close, I try to smile. Hating myself.

And she comes into the room then, our little daughter, pushing open the door and padding over to the bed and demanding that I open my eyes.

Leave mummy alone, she's not very well, her father says.

But she stands there anyway, breathing through her mouth and holding up a picture she's made – holding it right close up to my face – a frantic, crayoned picture showing three people hanging out of a boat on a choppy sea. And I ask her what it is and she says it's her other family.

What other family? I say.

The other one, she says. The one that you and daddy don't know.

Three days later, my head and body still weak and feverish, we meet in a pub. I don't know why we do this, it's a bad choice – loudest of loud music playing, people out after work, most of them younger than us, none of them with anything to hide. Laughter. Shouting. He is tired. I am tired. We feel old – we are old, look at us. We don't know what we're doing here. We don't do anything. We stand and we stare at each other's faces and we hardly even talk, we don't say a word, and then we part and return, each to our separate homes.

What am I doing? I think.

Two days go by. Two days of silence. I am almost relieved. Perhaps this is it, I think. Perhaps we've done all there was to do. Perhaps it's over now.

But then he sends me an email.

I don't know what to do about you. I didn't expect to love you like this. What I mean is, I thought I knew what my life was.

I thought I knew what my life was, too, I say.

Tell me what to do, he says.

SHORTLY BEFORE YOU LEAVE OUR HOUSE for what turns out to be the last time, an old friend of yours calls us. You've known this boy a long time, ever since nursery, in fact, though we didn't know that you still saw him much. And he claims to be very concerned about you, this boy does. He doesn't know how much we know – he realises it's quite possible that we know nothing, he says – but he tells us he'd never be able to live with himself if he didn't say something, do something.

Not long afterwards – inevitably, I suppose – you accuse this boy of having a far more serious and long-standing problem than you do. Because why else would he want to grass you up like this? We ought to know, you say, that he lies to absolutely everyone. His parents, for instance, are completely in the dark about his habit.

In the long ago days of nursery and play dates and sleepovers, we saw a lot of this boy's parents and got along OK with them, though I wouldn't say we were ever close. But now, when we ask if we can meet for a chat about the kids, they decline. Sorry, but they have no time right now. Work is frantic. They are frantic. No, they can't come round for a drink. And anyway they don't really see what there is to talk about.

They make it clear, when your father presses them, that they aren't at all worried about their boy. Sure, the allowance they give him does seem to disappear pretty fast these days. But no, they don't ask him what he does with his money, because they don't think it's any of their business. It's their belief that you can only interfere so much in your teenagers' lives before you run the risk of driving them away.

And though they concede that he's had his

problems – they were very disappointed when he gave up the cello, for instance – they're confident that he's a super-bright boy with a promising future ahead of him. He's just been offered a place at a good university. They're sure that as soon as he goes off there, away from all the bad influences, then everything will settle down.

When they say bad influences, they want us to know that they do not, of course, mean you, our daughter. But it isn't very hard, is it, to see that the two of you just aren't all that good for each other any more?

Probably just time they took a break from each other, they say. Perhaps the friendship has simply run its course.

YOU DO NOT HAVE A PLACE AT university. You've been bunking off school for most of the last year and, despite all the long and tearful talks, the threats and entreaties and bribes, the meetings with teachers and drawing up of contracts and filing of progress reports, you continue to turn up late or, sometimes, not at all.

You laugh when we say you should try and sit your exams anyway – that it doesn't matter what your grades are, that we really don't care, that all that matters is you finish school. You spend most of that final term out with various friends, frequently staying out all night, even though we try, repeatedly – pointlessly – to ground you.

I am aware, as I write it, of how weak this sounds.

You're living at home, with no job and no plans for the future. You do, briefly, work in an organic food shop but are fired after just three weeks when you swear at a customer. You seem to last even less time at the cafe, for reasons you're still hazy about.

You could of course think about college – so many times we've tried talking to you about that – but it would mean doing re-takes and right now you tell us you can't think of anything worse. When we ask you what you're doing up there all day in your room, you tell us that you're applying for jobs online, of course. Why? What else do we think you might be doing?

You rarely leave the house, but one night I find you in the hall with your parka on and a desperate look on your face. When I ask where you're off to, you scowl and tell me you're going to see him, your friend.

I ask you if you're going to his house.

Not his house, no.

Where, then?

You refuse to tell me.

Aren't I entitled to any kind of private life? you say.

When you return an hour later – eyes glittering, cheeks flushed – you accuse me of waiting up and spying on you.

I don't deny this. I tell you the truth – that I've been sitting here in the hall because I'm very worried about you.

A slow smile spreads over your face.

Why? What the fuck are you worried about?

I wish I knew.

You regard me coldly. But when I ask to see what you have in your coat, you give a bitter laugh and, lifting each hand in turn with exaggerated slowness, you watch as I feel around in your pockets.

You won't find anything in there, you say.

And you're right. I don't find anything. Just a pack of chewing gum, a hair elastic and some old receipts from the corner shop. You ask me if I've finished. And then you walk upstairs with a sour, vindicated smile on your face.

But later, when I knock on your bedroom door and you don't answer, I go in and find you curled on your bed, your knees pulled right up to your face. I sit down and lay my hand on your head. You're cold, damp and sweaty. Your face is wet, I can't tell whether with tears or sweat. I ask you if you're unwell. You don't say anything, you just shrug.

Come on, I say. Talk to me –

But you don't speak. For a while we do nothing, we stay there in the room and are silent together. At last I reach out and squeeze your shoulder.

Come on, I say again – and when you still won't say anything – You know, don't you, that dad and I would do absolutely anything to help you?

But you still don't speak. You remain very still, lifeless, even. If it wasn't for the steady pulse in your small thin arm, it might be possible to imagine that you aren't breathing.

LATER, THOUGH, YOU COME DOWNSTAIRS and open the fridge and, standing there in your T-shirt and knickers, you pour milk into a cereal bowl. Your undressed body is a shock. Your thighs are barely there, your elbows so sharp, the dip of your chest alarming.

I tell you I want you to see a doctor.

What?

Look at you – how thin you are. You never used to be that thin. I can tell you've lost a serious amount of weight.

Before you can say anything, your father comes in and, putting his bags down on the table, he asks you to please close the fridge door.

Why? – glancing at him as you continue to cram cereal into your mouth.

He regards you calmly.

Because when you stand there with it wide open like that, you're letting all the cold air out and wasting energy and that damages the planet.

Fuck the planet.

I beg your pardon?

And I look at him standing there and for a quick moment I can't help seeing him through your eyes – so righteous and steady and certain – and I wish I couldn't.

But when you spit at him – a mouthful of

milk-spattered cereal landing on his shoe – I'm as shocked as he is. It isn't, I suppose, such a big thing. Nothing like as frightening as the day three weeks ago when, asked to clean your room, you raised your fist and smashed it so hard against the landing window that the glass shattered and blood ran down your arm.

Not as depressing, either, as the day we confiscated your house keys and you pretended to be OK with it and we only later realised you'd stolen my own set from my handbag. I found myself locked out of the house for three hours on that bitter winter's day.

All the same, when your father turns to me, his face is alive with distress.

I can't live like this any more, he says.

ONE DAY, MEETING HIM FOR TWENTY UNSATISFACTORY minutes on a bench in the park, I tell him I know nothing about him. It is lunchtime. We're sitting in the rose garden. He is eating an apple with noticeable relish, his briefcase on his lap. He turns to me with the strangest look on his face.

How can you say that? You know absolutely everything about me. Everything important anyway.

I look at him.

But I don't even know your address.

This is true. I know which part of the city he lives in, but not where. Even after all this time, I don't know his wife's name or the names of his boys – precious details which he seems to guard from me very carefully.

I know the name of their dog, but only because he once let it out by mistake. It was the kids who named it, he was very quick to tell me, presumably because the name was surprisingly ordinary.

I know that he and his nameless wife like gardening, that they keep chickens, that they don't really think of themselves as city people, that they dream, sometimes, of moving to the country. His wife, he once told me, grew up in the country and would like to move back there.

And you? I said.

What about me?

Is that what you want? To live in the country?

He rolled his eyes.

I just do as I'm told, he said.

He tells me that they have a lot of parties, that they love entertaining. Or at least his wife does. Left to himself, he says he wouldn't do any of it. He likes to tell me that he's not as sociable as his wife is, and often, when he has to go home for a dinner, he'll complain that he isn't in the mood to see all of these people.

I wish I could just stay here quietly with you, he'll say.

Now, sitting here on this bench in the park with the scent of roses all around us, he flings the apple core into a bin and looks at his watch and asks me what I want to know.

You want my address? You can have my address. Seriously, he adds, I didn't realise it was so important to you. Of course I don't have a problem with you knowing where I live –

I tell him I don't want to know.

He looks at me carefully.

What I mean is, I trust you. It's not as if you're going to start turning up uninvited.

Would I ever be invited?

For a moment this question seems to unsettle him, but then he laughs.

What's the matter? he says as, keeping his eyes on my face, he takes hold of my hand, lifts it to his lips and kisses it. You know I don't want to keep things from you. Tell me you know that? You surely understand that I've always gone out of my way to be absolutely straight with you?

I say nothing.

Ask me anything, he says. Go on. I mean it. Ask me any question you like and I'll do my best to answer with absolute honesty.

I take a breath.

All right then, I say. What's she like, your wife?

He frowns.

What's she like? You mean what does she look like? I'm sure I've told you – fair hair, blue eyes, about your height –

No, I say, though in fact all of this is news to me. I

mean as a person? Is she funny? Is she kind? Does she make you laugh? Do you like her?

As I watch him think about this, my heart is racing. I'm not stupid. I know exactly what I've done. Even so, as I see his face soften, my blood turns to ice.

She's a good person, he says. And a wonderful mother. And yes, she's funny too, we have a lot of fun together. So I suppose if you're asking if I like her, the honest answer is yes.

A WILD-HAIRED AND DIRTY-LOOKING man comes up to me at a book festival. He has some copies of my novel in a carrier bag – perhaps ten or fifteen hardback copies – and he wants me to sign them for him. He just wants my name, he says, nothing else. He does not smile and he doesn't say please or thank you. All the time I am signing, he stands over me with his arms folded.

As I sign, I sneak some glances at him, the parts I can see anyway. He has on a dull green anorak, tracksuit bottoms and his trainers are caked with mud. The festival takes place in a series of tents in the middle of the countryside and, though they put down wooden planks whenever it rains, still if it's been very wet, you'll find yourself walking through mud at some point.

But this year it hasn't been wet. In fact the lack of rain has been very noticeable, everyone's remarked on it.

I sign all the books for this man. As soon as I've

finished, he grabs them back from me and, without a word, stuffs them back into the bag. Then out of another bag he produces a small camera.

I'm sorry, I tell him. I'd rather not be photographed.

What? – his eyes go wild with surprise.

I'm afraid I don't do photographs.

It'll only be a quick one –

I'm sorry.

I smile and try to catch the eye of the next person. The tent is hot and lively. My queue isn't long, in fact it's pitifully short, but I don't want to keep anyone waiting.

But the man does not move.

It'll just be a quick snap, he says – and he lunges towards me, raising the camera as if it's a weapon, holding it right in my face as if to show that he intends to take the picture whether I like it or not.

With my heart thumping so hard in my chest that my whole body seems to shake, I stand up and I raise my hand and, more loudly than I ever thought possible, I shout at him to leave me alone.

A moment of silence and then a murmur goes around the tent. People turning their heads, looking to see what's going on. An usher, a slender, dark-haired girl in a long skirt, hurries over and, touching the man on his sleeve, gently but firmly, asks him to leave.

But he does not leave.

Shoving her roughly out of the way, he turns back to me. For a single, awful moment I think he's going to do something crazy. Hit me. Or pull a knife from his bag. But instead, after fixing me briefly with his dark, upset eyes, he seems to lose energy. Muttering under his breath, he snatches up his bags and he strides from the tent.

Throughout all of this, you've been asleep at my feet – four months old, silent and sleeping in the carry-seat, mouth open, small, hot cheek pressed against the rabbit-patterned cushion. When I think about this fact – that you're here and the man was there, just a couple of feet away all this time, that I do not know what I'd have done if he had not decided to go – I feel as if the air has been punched out of me.

The usher, too, is shaken. She offers to fetch me a glass of wine and, while she's gone, the bookshop manager also comes over to see if we're both all right. Holding you in my arms now, I tell him we're fine.

But later, as I sit and feed you in the small, dark hotel room, I can't stop shaking.

And I think of how my mother told me that once, driving through the countryside with my brother and me in the back of the car, she found herself jumping the lights at a level crossing, hurrying her little blue Mini over the tracks just as the signal went and the lights turned to amber. She only just managed to clear the crossing as the barrier came down and the train went rushing past.

She told me she'd relived this moment many times

over the years. For such a long time it had haunted her, in fact she doubted it would ever leave her. Sometimes, even now, in the middle of the night, she'd feel it happening all over again –

The beep of the signal and the knowledge that the lights are changing, that the barrier is about to come down. And the fact that – for some reason she'll never be able to explain to herself – she just presses her foot down on the accelerator and, with two small children in the back, she forces herself to keep on going.

IT IS LATE AT NIGHT, I DON'T KNOW HOW late, and we are lying in the long, rough grass by the zoo. It is the end of summer, his wife has gone away with the kids, I told my husband I was going to meet a girlfriend for a drink, I should have been home two hours ago, I know that he'll call soon, so I've made sure to turn off my phone.

It's been a warm day but now the air is cooling, the sky streaked with pink. Faraway sounds of animals. The grass is damp. Dewy. He puts down his jacket and I lie down with my head on it and he lies on me, right on top of me as if we are teenagers, hip to hip, thigh to thigh, fitting his body to mine, pressing me down into the cool, damp earth, his lips on mine.

We kiss for a very long time.

At last he rolls off me and sits up, resting his head on

his hand. I look at him. He looks at me. We smile at each other. We do not speak. I reach for him, wanting to pull him back.

He doesn't let me. His face is suddenly complicated.

I don't think I can do it. I can't walk away from you, he says.

What, now?

No. No, any time.

Then stay –

I can't stay –

I want to be with you, I say.

He rolls over onto his back so I can't see his face. Looking up at the sky, draining of light. At last he sighs a long hard sigh.

We're going to have to do something about this, aren't we? he says. What I mean is, I can't make you live like this. It's not fair on you, not on me either. It's not fair on any of us.

My heart seems to still.

I'd do anything to be with you, I say.

I feel him glance at me. Then he takes hold of my hand. For a moment we lie there in silence staring at the huge, darkening sky.

I just don't see how we'd do it, he says at last. The logistics. What we'd do about all the kids, I mean.

I take a breath.

We'd work it out, I say.

You think so?

He rolls back towards me and he puts his arms around me and I say nothing, but we hold each other hard.

WE MEET AT A BAR, A PLACE WITH a corner dark enough for us to dare to hold each other. Soon, much too quickly, it's closing time. Out in the street we stand together, our two faces touching. He pulls my coat collar up around my ears, running his hands over my hair, catching hold of it, gathering it and holding it in his fist.

We tell each other that we must go home.

But we don't go home.

Instead we walk with our arms around each other, walking until we don't know where we are any more – these aren't even streets we recognise, we could be anywhere – and suddenly this does seem very funny. We start to laugh. We laugh for a long time and then he pushes me into the shadows and we kiss for an even longer time, such deep kissing that when we've finished, the sky is blacker than it was before. His eyes, too, very black.

In a bar full of people half our age, we have a last drink – the absolute last, we say – but I don't remember the drink, I don't remember anything except that at one point I get up and start to dance – surrounded by all those frantic, jostling bodies – and he watches me, leaning back with his arms folded and a small smile on his face. By the time we leave it's late, later even than we thought – the middle of the night in fact – and there are no cars anywhere and no hope of finding a taxi, so we walk until we reach a minicab office.

In the office, the man is drinking beer and watching sport on a high-up TV. At first he doesn't seem very interested in finding us a car, but we ask him again and then at last he finds us one. Turning up the volume on the TV, barely giving us a glance, he shrugs and tells us the car is outside waiting if we want to go.

We give our addresses – mine first – and then we glide on through those empty streets, nobody around now, and I think that I'm leaning against him, almost asleep, my head on his shoulder, stars and lights drifting by in the dark night air, and he says something to me but I don't hear it – I'm doing what I always do, gathering up my heart and getting ready to let go of him – and that's when we realise.

The car has slid off the road and turned into a yard next to what looks like a garage. Tyres piled up. Dustbins. A gate with a rusty padlock on.

Our driver has got out and is talking to someone.

Pushing me gently off his shoulder, he rolls the window down, suddenly sober now. I hear him asking the man what's happening.

What's going on? he says.

The man smiles a relaxed smile – almost sheepish, the smile is – and he holds out his hands and he explains that he wants money. For petrol. He can't take us any further, he says, unless we give him more money. He has no petrol. He needs the money right now.

He walks over to the car.

Now, he says.

I sit up. Stars moving fast in the black sky over my head. The world rearranging itself. Cold in my throat. I ask him where we are. He lays a hand on my wrist, shushing me.

It doesn't matter where we are, the man cuts in and his voice is rougher now. Can't go anywhere without the money.

He stays very steady. Getting out of the car and, keeping his eyes on the man, he digs in his coat. Taking out his wallet – how much? Is this enough? He gives the man the money and the man takes it. He looks at it. Folds it. He seems satisfied. He does not ask for more.

I think of my daughter back at home – safe and warm in her bed, arms flung above her head – and I begin to tremble.

Carefully, he puts his wallet away and then he gets back in the car. He seems relaxed, but he isn't relaxed. We don't look at each other. I am still shaking. What are we doing? Shouldn't we just get out of the car and go? It's dark and it's late, but my husband would do that, I know that he would. He would leave the car and the man and the money and take my hand and walk into the night, find a black cab, call the police perhaps. I don't know what he would do but I know that he would do something.

I whisper to him that we should get out of the car. But no, he shakes his head. His face is level. I don't know what he's thinking. He touches my hand again, firmly now, lacing his fingers through mine. The driver gets back in. He drives on. He does not stop for petrol. He drives.

Once we're close to where I live, we ask him to stop. He asks it. His voice is confident, reasonable, friendly.

Mate, thanks, anywhere here is fine.

And the car stops. Just like that, pulling in at the kerb. We both get out. I think the man even tells us goodnight.

Goodnight, we say.

My legs are trembling. I almost can't stand up. The car door slams. I think the man is smiling. We watch him drive away.

It is the beginning of the end. I don't know this then, but I do know it now.

TWO DAYS LATER, HE TEXTS TO SAY THAT he can't meet. Not today, not tomorrow, no, probably not even this week.

Panic rips through me.

Why? What's happened?

Can't talk about it, he texts. Got to go quiet for a while.

Quiet?

Can't go into any more detail – really sorry – nothing I can do. All v difficult.

What? I'm punching in the letters so quickly that my thumbs begin to shake. What do you mean? What's difficult?????

My phone rings. His voice. Cold.

Please just trust me. Just give me some time, OK?

What do you mean, time? How much time?

I wait for an answer, but he's not there any more.

Two weeks go by. Three. I think actually that it's more than three. Days and weeks and hours of pure agony.

I do what I have to do – I take my daughter to school, on play dates, trips to the park, driving to places in the car, strapping her in and out of the car seat, listening to all of her protests and chatter and doing my best to answer all the questions. I do all of this – feeding her, talking to her, taking care of her – but I might as well not be there because I am not a mother, not any more, I am no one –

The air around my child's head is strangely blank. Often I turn my eyes in her direction and find myself looking straight through her.

Coming down the stairs, one step at a time, sticky fingers on the bannister, she is calling and shouting for me.

I'm tired, I say. Please, I'm tired, leave mummy alone for a bit?

Quiet, it's all I want, just some time to be alone and quiet in this darkness.

She sits up in bed, lining up all her toys – the monkeys and bears and the various nameless and shapeless furry creatures – and introducing them to each other. It's a tea party, she cries. Look, mummy, a tea party!

Telling me to look at them.

I am looking, I say.

Fury goes over her face.

You're not, mummy. You're not looking! Do it now! Do it with your real eyes.

MY HUSBAND WANTS TO KNOW what the matter is.

The matter?

You look like a ghost, he says.

His face is hard. These days he always has it, the hard, hungry look of someone who knows he's being lied to.

I tell him it's nothing. I'm tired, that's all. And for once, this is not a lie. I am tired – heart tired, brain tired – so very, very tired.

His face hardens again.

You shouldn't be tired, he says. What have you been doing, to be so tired?

What have I been doing? If I was a less frightened person, I might laugh.

Sitting in the car at the traffic lights, I lift my hands and look at them, turning them around and around.

The fingers are flat, the skin white. I am colourless, formless.

He's right. A ghost.

Or perhaps a sea creature, drifting along on the sea bed, long and slow and smoothly translucent, barely visible in the deep water.

One morning right after the school run, I come home and I put myself on the bed, gazing down at the thick pile of the carpet, the small scuffs on the skirting board. I can no longer tell where the room ends and I begin.

Is there any more of me than this?

I pick my daughter up from school and take her to her swimming lesson – dressing and undressing her, getting the water wings on, pinching the valve and blowing the air in, sitting there on the chlorine-smelling bench at the shallow end, watching her shriek and laugh and wave. Pulling the belt of my coat tight, lifting my hand now and then –

It seems to work.

Mummy! Look! Mummy! – showing me that she can put her face in the water.

I smile. Shame crashing over me.

Like this, time passes.

A MONTH GOES BY. MORE THAN A month. One afternoon my husband comes home from the office early to find me sitting alone in the dark. Our daughter is at a play date. He asks me what I'm doing, sitting there with no lights on. I lift my head and look at him. For a moment nothing about him seems familiar. I put my hands to my face. Are there tears there?

I'm lost, I tell him.

He nods.

I know that, he says.

For a moment he stays, waiting there in the doorway. And then at last, very quietly, he crosses the room, putting down his coat and his briefcase and coming to sit down next to me. Wary as if he is dealing with a wild animal – putting a hand on me, his hand on the sharp top of my knee. Listening to his breathing, I am intent – waiting and waiting for him to say something, but still he doesn't speak.

At last he reaches over, turns on the lamp – letting the room burst softly into colour.

I don't know what you want from me, he says. I don't know how to be around you. I don't even know if you like me any more.

I say nothing. I don't know the answers to these things either. But when at last he puts his arm around me – very carefully as if my bones might break if he so much as squeezes – I feel myself move against him, breathing in the good kindness and warmth of him, settling despite everything, despite myself.

We sit like that until our daughter is dropped back home.

When at last – I don't know how long it's been but probably getting on for six or seven weeks – he texts me, I am not expecting it. I stare at my phone for a moment, waiting I suppose to feel something, but I don't think I feel much of anything. Actually, I don't have to think very hard. As if I had always known I'd do it – had planned to do it – I delete the text and I don't reply.

Though I do think about the text all that day and all of the next.

A couple of days later, he tries again.

Please, he says. He misses me. He can't begin to tell me how much he misses me. He has so much to say. Important things, things he can't possibly put in an email, he needs us to meet –

No, I say.

He writes again.

And again.

No.

Just a cup of tea. Ten minutes? He names a cafe, a place we've been to before.

I need it, sweetheart. Come on. Just so I can know where I stand – just so that you can tell me to go to hell, if you want to, he says.

AFTER MY MOTHER LEAVES MY father, we're walking in the park with my brother and the man who – though we don't know it yet – will soon be our stepfather. And perhaps I'm suddenly feeling very happy, because I slip my hand in his.

My mother stares at me. What do I think I'm doing? You're much too old for that, she says.

I'm embarrassed – shocked and dirty and embarrassed. I am twelve years old, skinny and mousy, my hair in a pigtail down my back. Hot, ashamed, I pull my hand away. I keep on walking. I never touch him again.

A few years later, my stepfather leaves my mother for another woman who has children around the same age as my brother and me.

My mother is distraught, inconsolable, crying and drinking and smoking. Her life is over, she says.

Soon after he leaves, my stepfather invites me round to the place where he and this woman and her children are living. Without telling my mother, I get on the bus and I go.

We sit together on brand new loungers on his unmown front lawn and he tells me how very sorry he is, that he wasn't able to go on living with my mother. It wasn't for lack of trying, he says. But sometimes these things just don't work out, you know.

He wants me to know that he wishes her well and hopes that once she's stopped being angry with him, she'll be able to rebuild her life. He hopes, too, that once the dust has settled, he can continue to have a relationship with my brother and me.

You two mean an awful lot to me, he says.

It's a hot day. I've just got my period and the lounger still has its polythene wrapping on and it sticks to my thighs. I am nauseous. My stomach hurts. I am terrified of leaking blood onto the lounger.

My stepfather asks me if I'm OK. I tell him I'm fine. He asks me what I'm thinking and I tell him I'm not thinking anything. And at that moment the new woman's car comes crunching onto the drive.

I don't see him for many years after that.

But when you're born, I write to him, inviting him to lunch. He replies immediately, a long letter, written in biro on blue paper. Just the sight of his familiar handwriting gives me a warm, tired feeling. He says that he's thought of me often over the years and misses me very much.

And he comes to lunch and he brings a bottle of champagne and he sits in the chair in the kitchen and holds you in his arms and I'm amazed at how normal it all feels, as if he's never been gone, as if he really is your real grandfather.

But when my mother discovers he's visited, she tells me how hurtful she finds it, that I went behind her back like that and contacted this man who, after all, lied to her and deceived and cheated on her for well over a year.

Almost eighteen months, he was seeing this woman. And all that time she'd thought he was just playing squash.

You don't know what a broken heart feels like, she says. And I hope for your sake that you never find out.

I write to my stepfather and tell him that I don't think it will work.

I'm very sorry, I say. I will always think of you, but it's just not fair on my mother.

He writes back to say he understands.

He's an old man now, this man who used to be my stepfather, but he's still alive and he's still with the same woman. I know this because now and then I look her up on social media, unable to resist scrolling through all the many birthdays and holidays, gazing at the pictures of my long ago stepfather, holding a glass of wine or wearing a funny hat and laughing with his three new, middle-aged stepsons and their wives and children.

I say new, but of course they're not new at all. I have to remind myself that these unknown adult people have already been in his life for many more years than I ever was.

Most of their lives, in fact. And they probably love him just as I loved him.

I'm sure they do.

YET AGAIN, YOU SAY THAT YOU NEED TO SEE us very urgently. As usual you're in big trouble, the worst kind of trouble, far worse than any kind of trouble you've been in before. I don't know what age you are by now but I know that time has passed and we have hardened. We find it very hard these days to get excited.

It'll be money, says your father.

Of course it will, I say.

It's a rainy night, dark, wet, cold. The pub is crowded. For once, you arrive on time. Your eyes are hard and your jaw set. Your father asks you what you want to drink. When you say you don't want anything, he goes to the bar anyway and gets you an orange squash.

While he's getting it – his face heavy as he holds out the money, trying to get the man's attention – I ask you how you are. A flash of pure malice goes through your eyes. Undeterred, I have a good look at you.

The clothes you have on – filthy, creased – seem to be the same as last time we saw you. Only the jacket is unfamiliar, not like something you'd wear. Your rucksack, which you place on the table in front of us, has a bad smell, rank, like meat. Your eyes are shining and not in a good way. Nothing about you is good or hopeful or pleasant. It occurs to me that if I had not actually given birth to you, I would move away.

The squash comes in a tall glass with a straw. You pick up the straw and put it in your mouth and chew on it viciously, but you push the drink aside. What happens next is no more than we expected. You demand money. Rattling off some facts, none of which make any sense or sound at all true.

You left your bag on a bus and lost everything. Which bag? Not this one. Someone unzipped the pocket of your bag and robbed you. No, of course you don't know how it happened. You must have fallen asleep. Or else the money just fell out, or –

Three hundred pounds – that's how much it was. How come you had the money? You ran an errand for a friend, didn't you, and you were on your way to give it to them, when you were robbed. Now you're in trouble, serious trouble. You don't know what will happen if you don't pay it back.

When we are not especially responsive to any of this, you push your chair back from the table. You seem to be about to stand up.

If you don't get the money right now, you say, if we won't take you straight from here to a cash machine – for surely we can see that you don't have time to sit around talking to us in this pub? – then bad things will happen.

Your father looks at you calmly. He picks up his drink.

What bad things?

You make a noise of fury.

Of course you can't tell us that. Are we saying that we don't believe you? Is this really what we want, to put you in such danger?

I sit up a little straighter.

What danger?

You glare at me.

I have texts. Threatening texts. I'll show you if you like. Though I have to warn you you might find them rather upsetting –

Your father folds his arms.

Show us.

What?

Show us the texts.

Now you grow properly furious. Are we really going to sit here and accuse our own daughter of lying? Do we really have to know every single fucking detail before we'll lift a finger to help you? If you loved me, you say, you'd just do it. I know you would. You'd help.

You burst into tears then and lay your head on the table. I stare at you – looking at the back of that head of yours, your so-familiar hair, the strange little whorl on the crown near your parting which has been there ever since you were a baby.

You sob into your arms. The noise is loud, persuasive. People are turning around and looking at you. But when you lift your head, your eyes are dry.

You cannot think of a single friend, you say, whose parents would not do this for their child.

Hearing this, your father just smiles at you.

You stay in the pub for less than five minutes after that. Once you know that it's hopeless, once you know you're getting nothing from us, then the dead kind of flatness in your voice disappears and you start to yell. The kind of noise that few people would allow themselves to make in a public place.

You accuse us of tricking you. Of luring you here under false pretences. Whatever happened to unconditional love? You want us to know, by the way, that you blame us for every bad thing that has ever happened to you, every time you've been in danger, every moment of fury and sadness and pain, your absolute lack of chances in life, everything – and you still can't believe that we don't care the slightest bit about your safety.

At last your father puts down his drink and pushes back his chair.

If you're genuinely in danger, then this is a matter for the police –

The police? You want to call the police?

If what you're saying is true, yes.

You almost spit at him.

You should be ashamed of yourselves as parents –

We could just tell you the truth – that we are ashamed of ourselves as parents, that you will probably never know or understand how intensely ashamed we are.

But we don't say this. Instead, once the rant has finished, I hear myself tell you that you're full of shit.

I am stunned. It isn't even something I'd say. Shit. It isn't a word I'd use. And yet you are, aren't you?

Full of shit.

Not a single thing you've told us is true. Not a word, not a sentence, every single utterance is a lie calculated to extract money from us.

Most of all, though, you are high.

She's right, your father says when I tell you this. You must have used before you came here.

Your eyes turn black with rage. You deny it

immediately and with a fury. And then just as quickly and hotly you admit it.

Why do you think I use? you scream at us. Has it never occurred to you that I have to get off my fucking head before I can come anywhere near you two?

And you pick up your bag and, knocking over your chair as you stand, you leave. People in the pub getting out of your way fast, watching you as the door swings open and shut – a cold wind blowing through.

Your father leans over to pick up the chair. Looking down at the table, at your untouched drink. A patch of wet where the drinking straw has been left, bent and twisted and chewed, as if a malign and terrible force has just passed through this place –

He asks me if I'm all right. I tell him I'm fine. We're about to go, but then we agree that we should wait a moment or two, just in case you come back. Even though we both know you won't come back, still we wait –

Five minutes.

Your father checks his watch.

He checks it twice.

When after seven minutes there's still no sign of you, we get up and we leave.

I REFUSE TO MEET HIM AT NIGHT, TEA IS the best I can do, I say. So we meet in the middle of the afternoon, in a cafe in the rain. The sky is black, the pavements wet. I think that he looks very well, his face calm and rested, his fair hair longer and softer. He actually looks as if he's been on holiday, something he immediately denies when I ask him. You really think I get time for holidays? he says, reminding me that his wife always has to take the kids away without him.

He glances at his watch and I ask him how much time he's got. He throws me a serious look and then he smiles.

I can stay as long as I want, he says.

You haven't got to get back?

Not today, no.

I ask him, then, what it was that happened, the thing that meant he couldn't see me these past few weeks.

His face stiffens.

It's not something I can talk about.

Was it to do with your family?

He hesitates and then he nods.

In a way, yes, it was.

But what? What happened? Was someone ill?

With a sigh, he reaches out, puts a hand over mine.

Look, I'm sorry –

What? What are you sorry about?

He looks at me.

It's just that it involves other people –

Which people? Who does it involve?

He says nothing. Shakes his head. We both look over at the window, the rain running down it. I tell him that I cannot think of a single thing that could happen in my life that would cause me to withdraw contact so completely like that. Not from him. Not without even telling him what it was.

He gazes at me. His eyes are soft.

Nothing at all? he says. You can't think of anything?

I look at him for a moment.

No, I say.

He looks away. Outside the rain is coming down harder. People are coming into the cafe with their bags held over their heads. The door opens and closes again, wet gusts of air coming in.

I love you, he says, turning back to me. I have always loved you, do you know that? I don't think there has been a single second of a single year since the first time I met you that I haven't felt love for you.

I look at him, watching the shape of his mouth as he says this.

Yes, I say.

What does yes mean?

You don't love me.

He shakes his head, takes a breath.

You were so lovely, you know. When you were seventeen, so happy and open to everything – you had this little spark inside you – everybody saw it, it wasn't just me. How could I not have loved you?

I hold myself very still.

I don't recognise that person, I tell him.

Of course you do. She's here right now.

She isn't.

I can see her.

No, you can't.

He is silent for a long moment then – looking out of the window, as if searching for a clue to his next move. When he turns back to me there are tears in his eyes. They look like real tears. He looks down at his hands in his lap.

Will you go to a hotel with me? he says.

THE YOUNG WOMAN I'VE BEEN teaching emails me. She says she hopes I don't mind her writing but she just read another of my novels, the one about the affair with the narcissistic and controlling married man. And she hasn't been able to get it out of her head, in fact she's really been quite shaken up by it.

It reminded me of so many things, she writes. I suppose it reminded me, in a rather terrible way, of me. I had a relationship so exactly like that a few years ago and it brought it all back. That guy, the way he manipulates her. My god. It was like you were looking into my mind at times. I have to say that I found it incredibly unnerving to read.

For a moment, I struggle to remember which book she's talking about. I must have written it at least fifteen years ago, perhaps even more. I do have a dim memory of the process: the room, the single window with its view of the car park and the dustbins – you were small and I was renting an office down the road from our house at the time.

I remember the smell of cheap new carpet, the long days of drinking instant coffee – cup after cup, each one going cold – and staring at the wall. The fact that the book was not easy to write, that it seemed, for some reason, to suck out every atom of my mental and physical energy. Sometimes, even between getting the paragraphs out, I had to lie down on the floor for several minutes with my eyes shut.

I ate a lot of chocolate during that period. Chocolate, and instant mashed potato – a throwback to childhood caravanning holidays and something that always made your father laugh.

Later, I got a blood test. It turned out that my iron levels were low.

The book didn't get good reviews –the best you could say is they were mixed. It didn't sell either, or not much anyway. I did have a lunch with a young film director who was briefly interested in the rights, but it all came to nothing. Once I'd finished doing all the readings, I don't think I ever picked it up again.

I hope you don't mind my asking, my student writes in her email, but I wondered where it all came from – what I mean is, what was it based on – did you make it up or was it at all autobiographical? That guy, I felt I almost knew him, he just seemed so real. And the way it was written, too. I know it's a novel, but it didn't feel like one. It felt more like a memoir – something about how direct it was – it almost felt like a confession at times.

I suppose I was wondering if that was a conscious thing? Please don't feel you have to answer if you don't want to, she adds.

I TELL MY HUSBAND THAT WE HAVE to separate. I tell him this on a bright blue autumn day when, because he's not due into the office till ten, he's taken the chance to drop our daughter at school.

It's not your fault, I tell him, it's my fault. I've done things that I can't live with, I can't continue living like this any more.

I tell him a few other things too, some of them true, others less so.

He is baffled, confused, he is furious.

I thought we were finally getting back to normal, he says.

After I tell him all these things, he doesn't go to work at all. He calls in sick and tells his secretary to cancel everything and then he slams a plate down so hard on the kitchen counter that it breaks and after that we have a long talk.

When he breaks the plate, I'm almost happy. I want things to break. I think about my father after my mother left him – how for a while, he broke almost everything he could get his hands on – and now when my husband breaks the plate, I am glad of the damage, glad to have a reason to hate him.

We ask a friend to collect our daughter from school and give her tea. We are still talking as the light leaves the sky.

When my husband speaks, he does not look at me. He can't look, not now, not after I've done this to him, not any more. I can tell that he thinks I am far too cruel to be looked at, too callous and untrustworthy. He says that he hates the way I speak to him, he hates what I am doing to him, he does not trust me, he knows that I lie to him.

He knows this.

That I lie.

Of course he does.

How could I ever have imagined I'd get away with it?

He is so very ashamed of the person I've become that – and I see this now – he has developed a whole new face and posture for dealing with it. A new and upsetting way of holding himself – of folding his arms in a tense way and licking his lips before he speaks. As if he's dealing with a mad person, as if he must measure every step that he takes. The expression in his eyes says that he must be wary, that I cannot be trusted. That tells me, actually, that he would rather be anywhere than here with me.

But he does not see why our marriage should have to end.

I still love you, he says.

Love. Still. Apparently it really is that simple.

We talk about this for two whole days. We talk about what we have done to each other, with each other, what we might still do together. The past, the future, the present. We talk about our child. And when we talk about her, that's the only time that I find I can't do it – feeling myself falling wide open, I cry, I can't help it, the sobs come heaving out.

Love.

And I see him looking at me then, and I know what he's thinking. He's wondering how I can claim to feel love for our child, while calmly disposing of her family like this.

I tell him that I am very sorry, and it's true, I am so sorry. How could I do this? How could I have done it? I used to be a good person. I did try to be. It is in most ways a mystery to me how I got myself to this place.

Have you slept with him? he says.

No, I say.

Is that the truth?

I don't know, I say, even though it is. I don't want to lie to you –

But you do lie to me.

I do, yes.

That night, we startle each other by making love.

Ferocious, untender, unlovely yet surprisingly satisfying love. Afterwards, as if we don't care what happens next, we lie in each other's arms and we sleep.

And then at last he seems to accept it. That we are over. Drawing in his claws. Meek. Agreeing. It is quite a shock to me, when he agrees. Saying that he'll go along with whatever I want, that I am almost certainly right.

It will all be OK, he says.

Will it?

Yes, it will.

Right, I think.

And suddenly just like that, it is over. We are over. And it feels terrible, far more easily done than I thought it would be.

The days pass. I notice that he's pale. He does not shave. He loses weight. He sweats. Sometimes, pouring the coffee, his hand shakes.

I lock myself in the bathroom and I cry.

It's my fault, I tell him. I have done this to us.

You've done it to yourself, he says and I am frightened by how mild and forgiving his face is. But I don't blame you for it. I just think it will be better for our little girl if we are not together.

That sentence, coming from his mouth, destroys me.

I tell him we must do this amicably, that we must put you first. I tell him I've taken some advice, even though I have not taken any advice.

He knows, after all, that I lie to him.

He tells me that he is very sorry.

Sorry for what?

I don't know, he says.

We lie in bed together and he holds my hand, gripping my fingers in his, stroking my hand. I let him do it, in fact I fall asleep like this, still holding onto his hand. I wonder if all people who are separating cling to each other like this.

The moon outside our bedroom window is enormous, a perfect globe of white like in the nursery rhyme.

I'm so miserable, I tell him.

He touches my head.

I know, he says.

ON THE NIGHT THAT YOUR FRIEND – THE ONE that you've known since nursery – finally calls to tell us what's going on, we're sitting on the lawn. It's unusual for him to call your father's mobile – I'm not sure we even knew that he had the number. But of course your father takes it. I'll always have time for that boy, he said recently, whatever those idiot parents of his think of us.

The last few weeks with you have been especially difficult. Your moods are increasingly unpredictable, you're angry and aggressive, you frighten us sometimes – sobbing and shouting, threatening us and breaking things. Other times you just sleep – going to bed and staying there, waking up later with a bleak, child-like look on your face.

The psychiatrist you're seeing has told us to be patient. She sees a lot of cases like yours and nothing is set in stone. She has got you onto a different set of meds. She's optimistic. You'd be surprised by how quickly things can change, she says.

It is warm out in the garden, a perfect summer's evening. Wood pigeons flapping in the trees above us, cooking smells drifting from the flats across the road. I've been dead-heading and my fingers have the warm and peppery smell of geraniums. We've opened a bottle of wine. I think that, despite everything, on this particular evening, we're feeling OK.

At first, your father talks to your friend in his normal, relaxed way. But after a moment or two, I notice that something's changed. His voice begins to falter and slow. At last, instead of speaking, he begins to listen. For a very long time after that, he says nothing at all. I watch as his face grows still.

I take a sip of my wine. Keeping my eyes on his face. His darkening face. Trying to work out what the boy can possibly be saying to make your father look so serious.

My attention is only half on him. My mind's relaxed, now and then floating off around the summer garden, taking in the stillness and the warmth and the air, before returning again to your father's face.

And that's when it dawns on me that he doesn't look at all happy. Also that this boy – who never normally has much to say – must be talking and talking because your father hardly says a thing.

Just yes and no, and OK, right, and oh, I see.

At last he lets out a long sigh. And, shutting his eyes for a moment, he says something which changes everything, which opens a bright cavern of pain in my chest.

How long do you think she's been using? he says.

Four

DURING THAT PERIOD OF TIME – IT is less than four weeks, but feels like so much longer – when I have to take you into the chemist every day, we are always served by the same people. The plump girl with the curly hair and the birthmark on her neck. The quiet-faced young woman in a hijab. And the manager guy in the short-sleeved white shirt and tie who always looks tense and bad-tempered, but is actually meticulously kind in a way that anyone but you would be able to understand.

It is first thing in the morning and – pulled from your bed with a hoodie thrown over your pyjamas and your feet stuffed into trainers – you're not feeling good. Your mouth is dry and your whole body aches. They say it's like the flu, this feeling. Or no, worse than the flu. Like the worst flu anyone can imagine, with a whole lot of other things thrown in, that's what you say. Certainly, it puts you in the foulest of moods. But maybe that's understandable. You wouldn't drag a person who has flu halfway down the street and make them queue in a shop for their medication.

Still, you're not very co-operative. You don't like that they have to watch you swallowing the pills, to see you actually put them in your mouth and wash them down. You don't appreciate this at all. It feels like an insult, you say, an infringement of your human rights.

Why can't they just trust you?

What else are you going to do with your medicine, except put it in your mouth?

Better still, why can't they just give you a prescription like any normal fucking person? A prescription that I, your mother, could go out and collect for you, so that you wouldn't have to heave yourself out of bed first thing every fucking morning when it ought to be clear to anyone with half a fucking brain that you so badly need to sleep.

Because, you see, you don't think that you're the kind of junkie who should have to queue up with the other junkies for your medication. Even though until quite recently, you lay on a filthy bed in a filthy squat waiting for a fix along with the rest of them. Even though you have, at one time or another, sold your body or stolen steaks, vodka and anything else you can slide under your jacket at the supermarket, in order to sell them to raise enough money to inject yourself several times a day, still you are taking it very badly that you have to do this now.

The partitioned-off cubicle next to the pharmacy counter is supposedly there for the privacy of the patients, but it isn't a pleasant place. Someone has decided to carpet it – a mistake, we both agree, since the smell of urine is strong. There are brownish smears on the walls. The single chair is spilling foam from its grubby vinyl seat, where it's been mended in many places with silver duct tape.

You always sit on this chair while I stand. Neither of us ever questions this need of yours – this right, almost – to take the chair. I am older than you, exactly thirty years older, to be precise. And I haven't been well lately. So I'm not sure why it is that you're the one who sits and I'm the one who stands. If your father knew about this, he wouldn't be pleased, in fact I know he'd say it was ridiculous, my giving in to you like this. He'd tell me that, just on principle, I should insist on having the chair.

But your father doesn't know. And anyway it's first thing in the morning and I do believe that, on the whole, you're feeling worse than I am today. And I'm your mother and, like all mothers everywhere, it would never once occur to me to do anything other than put the needs of my sick child first.

Also, I don't really fancy sitting on that chair.

Sometimes, in the chemist's, we have to wait for a very long time while they sort the prescription out. This is partly because they're dealing with a lot of other people at the same time – not just junkies but normal people with their normal and innocently acquired ailments. But it's also because you have to be given a little bit less medication every day – by the time you leave to go away you'll hopefully be receiving almost nothing – and this has to be very carefully calibrated.

And, as I said, you aren't happy. You find the waiting very tedious. You roll your eyes and grumble and sigh and refuse to answer me when I speak to you. And you speak in such a rude voice to the staff. Actually that's the worst thing – the thing that upsets me the most. I get an almost physical pain in my chest when I hear you speaking to those people in such an insolent and offhand way.

I beg you to please at least try and be nice.

But you aren't nice. Sticking out your long skinny legs in the trainers which I bought for you last year without telling your father – because I could not bear your feet to be so wet, but also, let's be honest, because I wanted, more than anything, for you to talk to me – and which are now filthy and broken from your life on the street. You fold your slender arms which, even on the hottest days, are still covered in the longest of long sleeves to hide the marks where you've hurt yourself, and you close your eyes.

I watch your face – so very imperious, entitled, resigned. Your lashes are wonderfully silky and dark, your skin so flawlessly youthful, creamy as a flower in bloom. Despite everything you've done to yourself, I have to admit that you are still pretty much perfect – a dazzling specimen of youth and beauty – and I think you know it. You have the look of an exotic and haughty young emperor waiting for his retinue of courtiers to shape up.

And yet, however rudely and truculently you behave, however much you sigh and frown and snap, you are always treated with the utmost dignity and tact by those kind people at the chemist.

WHEN AT LAST YOU LEAVE TO GO TO rehab, I take these people a box of chocolates. It seems like the least I can do – a big and showy box, the biggest I can find, in dark, luxurious packaging, with a bow on top. I take it in that very same morning, as soon as I've seen you off to get the train with your father. The reason I do it immediately is partly because it does suddenly seem very urgent. But I think it's also because I suspect it will be a very long time before I'll be able to face that chemist's shop again.

I write a message on the little card that comes with the box. I write that the chocolates are to thank the staff for all their kindness. Not only to you, my daughter, but to me as well. Every day, every morning, such constant patience and understanding and generosity they've shown us. And you can't know until you've been through something like this what a difference other people's kindness makes.

Smiles, patience, a gentle look in someone's eye. A comment about the weather or the length of the queue, to show solidarity, to indicate that we are, all of us, in the exact same boat when it comes to the difficult and unlikely things that this life of ours dishes out. Small things, perhaps, but they can make all the difference between a situation which is unbearable and one which is – just about – tolerable.

I don't think I understood this when I was younger. I probably didn't even understand it a few years ago. But I definitely understand it now.

All the same, I know that I blush very hard when I hand the box of chocolates over. As a gift it seems both far too much and nowhere near enough. And this fact embarrasses me. And the manager in the short-sleeved shirt also seems embarrassed. For a moment, actually, he seems quite taken aback – both of us embarrassed, for ourselves and for each other – which of course only makes things worse.

But he also can't stop smiling.

Standing there at the till with the box of chocolates – letting it sit on the counter among the cough sweets and the indigestion remedies – he smiles and smiles. And after the serious-faced young woman in the hijab has come over and he's shown her the chocolates and she's examined the card and turned it over and admired the little rosebud on the front and she too has thanked me in her grave and careful way, he tells me that he wants me to know that he wishes you well, they all do.

He says that he can see that you are a very good girl, a nice girl. A lively girl, he says, smiling at me, certainly very full of personality. He's sure that you'll do very well in life, that you'll go far. He wants me to know that he and all the staff at the chemist wish you all the best.

He asks me if I think you might go off to uni once you're well again.

Uni. I blush again.

And I tell him – blurting this part out in such painfully imprecise sentences – that we really hope so, your father and I, that more than anything in the world, we'd love for you to go back into education.

But for now, I say, nothing is certain. She needs to recover first. We're just trying to take things a day at a time.

Baby steps.

Because that's what life has taught us. That there isn't much point in planning ahead. Because none of us can really know what life will throw at us next.

And the man seems to listen very carefully to this. He nods and he smiles and then he tells me something which both at that moment and for a long time afterwards – especially in the days and weeks and months that follow – brings tears to my eyes.

He tells me that I'm a very good mother.

He says that my daughter is very lucky to have a mother like me, she really is.

And the young woman in the hijab looks at me and she nods in her calm, unsurprised way, as if this is something that is absolutely taken for granted – perhaps even something they've already discussed –

I am a very good mother.

Definitely.

There seems to be no question at all about it in their eyes. It does not seem for one moment to have crossed either of their minds to think that I might be a very bad mother indeed – neglectful, selfish, frightened and chaotic, that I might have spent years putting my own appetites and interests and emotions first – that I might even possibly be to blame for this appalling and tragic mess you are in.

I WAIT ON A BENCH BY THE ZOO, NOT all that far from the place where he once lay on top of me in the long grass, pressing his body into mine. It's a blustery day, the skies heavy, animal cries tearing the air.

I sit alone for a long time, but at last, almost as if by accident, he comes walking up.

He has on a long coat, his winter coat, probably the

coat he was wearing when I first ran into him that time so long ago. His face, too, is wintry, his expression pinched and serious. When he sits down next to me, he does not touch me. Keeping his hands on his knees, he asks me how I am.

I tell him I'm fine. Pulling my coat a little tighter around me.

He doesn't waste any time. He tells me that he got talking to his wife at the weekend, that they ended up having a very honest conversation. It took him by surprise, actually, how honest and heartfelt it was.

And, well, a lot came out of it, he says.

I look at him. A dead feeling going through me.

What came out of it?

He takes a breath, rubbing his hands together, placing them back on his knees.

Well, for a start, I suppose I tried to be honest. For the first time in a long time, I made myself tell her the truth. I felt it was the least I could do, really. She's my wife, after all. I felt I at least owed her that.

You told her the truth about what?

He glances at me.

Well, I told her how I feel about you, for one thing.

I lift my head, surprised.

You told her that?

I feel him hesitate.

I did, yes. I told her how extremely fond of you I am.

Fond. My blood slows.

I explained that you mean an awful lot to me – that our friendship has always meant a lot. I did go out of my way, actually, to make sure that she knew that –

Friendship.

Several things go through my mind: the small pink and grey hotel near the station where, having taken the key from the woman at the desk, we stood so very close together in the lift, breathing and not touching, just breathing, staying with the moment which we'd been circling around for such a long time. Standing in the room and pulling the blinds down, the defeated, almost beaten look of his head as he sat down on the bed. The shock as we came together, the clean, dark pulse of his body through mine –

I swallow back tears.

You told her we were friends?

I did, yes.

I snatch a look at his face. And I see that it's changed – it's a stranger's face, closed to me. I see that he's managed to turn off the one thing – whatever mysterious thing it was – that used to let me see inside of him.

I ask him if his wife understood, about our 'friendship'.

He takes a breath, leaning forwards with his wrists on his knees. Appearing to consider this, he is silent for a long moment and then at last he sighs.

I don't know – I don't know if she understood or not. If I'm honest, I'm not sure that I ever expected her to understand. Why should she understand?

I nod. He's right. Of course he is. Why should she?

I didn't tell her everything, obviously.

You didn't?

No. Of course I didn't.

What did you tell her?

It doesn't matter what I told her, does it? The fact is – and I suppose this is what I didn't expect – it led to our having a very honest talk about our relationship, our marriage –

He keeps his eyes on the ground. I don't move. Holding myself very still –

He takes a breath.

It's a talk we should probably have had a long time ago. My fault, I'm sure. I take full responsibility. I think it's something that I've been avoiding. We've been married a very long time, you see – and then there are the boys, our boys –

He looks up at last, sees my face. The horror there – the certain knowledge that I don't want to hear about his big long marriage, or his responsibilities, or his boys.

I tell him it's OK.

You don't have to say anything else, I tell him. I understand.

And I think that's enough – it ought to be enough – but when he turns to me, his eyes are hard.

You say that – do you know, you often say that? – but you see, I don't think you do understand. Your relationship – your marriage – it isn't the same, from what you've said, it's different, isn't it?

What have I said? In what way isn't it the same?

He breaks off, seeing my face.

I'm sorry, he says. Forget I said that. It's not what I meant.

What, then?

I don't know.

You do know.

No, I don't.

For a moment we're both silent. At last I ask him what exactly he wants from me. What kind of understanding is it exactly that he wants?

He sighs. He doesn't speak. I shut my eyes, squeezing away the tears before they can come.

I've given you so much understanding, I say. I've tried to give you everything –

I know. I know you have.

He reaches for my hand, taking hold of it as if it's a thing that still belongs to him, pulling it into his lap, keeping it there between his two hands.

You're cold, he says. So cold.

I don't want anything from you.

All right.

I mean it. Nothing.

All right. All right, I know – he sighs, bowing his head, letting it hang there. For a long time, still holding onto my hand, he says nothing. What a mess, he says at last.

I withdraw my hand. That's it, I think, it's the last time I will ever touch him. And something inside me closes.

As if he senses this, he turns and looks at me.

I love you, you know. That part at least is true. I wasn't lying when I said I love you very much. I will always love you. You think it's not true, but it is, it's true.

THE READING ISN'T DUE TO START until quarter past, but already there are people sitting down. Almost all are women, one or two young, but most older. Some sit in pairs but others are alone, bags held on their laps, eyes fixed on the slightly raised area which will serve as the stage. Not a single one of them looks at me as I follow the young man who's the organiser down between the rows of chairs and past the trestle table where a young woman is setting up the books.

He takes me into a small room with a kettle and a sink and a dishcloth hanging over the tap. He explains that we're to wait in here until they're ready to start. Apologising for the fact that there's nowhere to sit, he leans against the sink and folds his gingery arms and yawns noisily. It's been a very long week, he says, and frankly he's knackered.

Pointing to where the toilet is, he asks if I'd like to use it.

Perhaps in a minute, I say.

He tells me that there's water out there on the stage – and by the way, he hopes I'm all right to read standing up at a lectern, but without a mic? Or would I rather sit? A chair can easily be provided, he says.

I tell him I'm fine to stand and he nods.

The acoustics aren't great in here. But most people seem to manage.

He explains that once he's introduced me, he'll leave me to read and talk. But he'll keep an eye on the time and then, once I've finished, he'll give me a hand with fielding the questions.

If there are any questions, he says. They've been quite vocal so far this year, but we get the odd event where they all just seem to clam up.

He adds that he ought, by the way, to apologise in advance for the fact that he hasn't read my novel, not properly anyway. But he's had a look at it and thinks it seems quite intriguing. And the reviews have been great, haven't they?

They've been OK, I say.

He smiles.

I might even get you to sign a copy for my other half – she's a big reader and she has a birthday coming up.

I begin to tell him that of course I'd be happy to sign one, but already his eyes have changed and he's scrolling through the messages on his phone. He tells me it's almost time, so if I want to use the toilet, now might be the moment.

*

THE HALL'S FILLED UP, THOUGH AS usual most people seem to have chosen the chairs furthest away from me. Trying to keep a smile on my face, I scan the rows, desperately hoping that I don't know anyone. The only other time I did a reading here – years ago, I think it was when my first book came out – one of my old teachers turned up. Or at least I was pretty sure it was her, but it was very hard to believe it because I was a middle-aged woman now, visibly aged and changed, and she looked no different at all.

And she sat through my event in such a still and unsmiling way, her lips pursed so exactly as I remembered them, a small frown between her brows. And I found this face of hers – the fact that it hadn't altered the smallest bit in all this space and life and time – so disconcerting that I ended up hurrying my reading, losing confidence and falling over my words in a rush to get the whole thing over and finished with.

I expected – dreaded – that she'd come up and try and talk to me at the end. But no, the moment the reading was over, she left, holding onto her tiny handbag and picking her way as quickly as she could through the plastic chairs towards the exit sign and the stairs. As I watched her go – narrow-shouldered and purposeful in her dark, belted raincoat – I was surprised by how diminished I felt.

Now the organiser stands and introduces me by saying how delighted the festival is to have tempted me back here to the place of my birth. He makes a couple of jokes about being relieved that I've never chosen to write about the place and I make a lame one back, saying, well, there's still time isn't there – and the audience laughs. The tension is broken, the room begins to relax. People uncross their legs and cough and one or two put their bags down on the floor.

But in the second row, not far from me, there's a woman who does not laugh. She doesn't even smile. If anything, her eyes only darken, her jaw becoming a little more set with each moment that passes. Her face is drawn and she looks tired, discouraged, even annoyed. Something about her makes me uneasy. I wonder if we were at school together.

But once things get going, I forget all about her. I do my best to sound lively and interesting, though as usual the more I talk, the less true it all begins to sound. But the audience are friendly and good-hearted and I answer a handful of questions. It isn't until the event is almost over that this woman puts up her hand.

And the question she asks isn't really a question at all. Instead she launches into a lengthy description of one of my earlier novels. She says that she didn't mind the violence – she reads a lot of crime and my work is pretty tame compared to that. But she didn't even slightly understand where I was going with the plot. It was extremely confusing at times, she says. And she hasn't a clue what was supposed to have happened at the end.

Was the woman alive or dead? Walking off across the beach like that –

She wondered for a moment if she was supposed to have committed suicide? Or was it just a metaphor for something? Either way it left her feeling very dissatisfied. And she has to admit that she's now more than two thirds of the way through this new one and finding herself equally frustrated by it.

I don't see why she'd bother with him – isn't it completely obvious from the start that he's playing with her? Would any grown woman really be so gullible? And it does all seem a tad too obvious, the part when she runs into him again all those years later and –

Laughing, the organiser lifts a hand: No spoilers please!

The woman ignores him.

And then what about the daughter? I must say I'm not finding any of the characters all that sympathetic, but I really can't begin to see why we're supposed to care about her. And the ending – again I suppose you'll just say it's left deliberately ambiguous, but some people might say that's called having your cake and eating it –

The organiser stands up. Running his hands through his hair and glancing at the clock, he asks the woman if this is her question.

Is what my question?

Well, you're saying you're confused?

She regards him stonily.

I'm not confused, no.

He tries to smile.

All right then, but you say you don't find the characters very sympathetic. But I'm wondering, do they necessarily need to be sympathetic?

The woman blinks.

If I'm going to be forced to read a whole book about them, yes.

A faint ripple of something goes through the audience. The organiser throws me a helpless look and sits back down. I take a breath and, trying to smile at this woman, I tell her I'm still not sure what the question is.

Her face hardens.

My question is, why do you write the way you write?

The way I write? You mean my style?

This need to write about such extreme things all the time and leave the reader in the dark about everything – she looks away briefly – I suppose I just don't get it, that's all.

My heart is thumping. I look at my water glass. I can't be sure that my hand won't shake, but I pick it up anyway.

Do I know you? I ask her, once I've taken a sip and put the glass back down.

What?

I'm just wondering if we've met before, that's all.

For a moment this seems to throw her. But then she tells me very firmly that she's never seen me in her life before. In fact, she says, she hadn't even heard of me until her book group suddenly did two of mine, one after the other. Not her choice, she hastens to add, but someone else's.

I tell her that two in a row does sound quite punishing.

A burst of nervous laughter from the audience. The woman's face does not change, but I notice with relief that she seems a little less able to hold my gaze.

I suppose they just weren't to my taste, she says.

ONE DAY, COMING HOME EARLY FROM somewhere or other, I find your father sitting in our kitchen with a woman. The two of them sitting very close together at the kitchen table – so close that their hands and wrists and elbows are almost touching.

And I know this woman. Not intimately – our friendship has never quite widened and softened the way some do. But she and her husband have been to ours and we've been to theirs and they're nice people, I've always thought so –

But I'm also in awe of her. Your father maintains he can't see it, but she has a mysterious kind of glamour, this woman does, with her unmade-up face and long hair openly streaked with grey, the plain, almost mannish clothes which I would never have the confidence to wear but which look so exactly right on her.

She doesn't talk much. She never seems to need to. She doesn't ever apologise for anything, or, as I do, anxiously fill gaps in the conversation with pointless questions and noises and observations. But she's one of those people you look for the moment you enter a room – there's so much going on in her face, her voice, her eyes.

But there's a night when they come to dinner and I take her long soft coat from her to hang it up and, carrying it through the hall, I can't resist putting my face in it, breathing in its heady, grown-up scent. But when I ask her what the perfume is, she seems taken aback – and then she tells me she's not sure she has any on.

And this disappoints me. It makes me feel that she can't be trusted. Because why would someone so effortlessly beautiful and charismatic need to dissemble like that?

And now, walking in here and seeing the two of them sitting there so close and quietly together, I don't know what to say. I can't think of any reason why they would both be sitting here like this, in the middle of the day. Why is your father not at the office? Why is this woman even in our house? Nothing about the situation is normal, but most surprising of all is that she's crying. Sitting there at our table with a cardigan around her shoulders and clutching a handful of tissues, her beautiful, interesting face wet with tears.

And when I come in, neither of them says anything. No explanation is offered. And the look on your father's face tells me everything I need to know.

*

I MEET UP AGAIN WITH THE YOUNG WOMAN I'M teaching. It's the last thing I feel like doing, but we've agreed that I'll read several pieces of her work in progress over a period of a few months and give her a total of three sessions. And – as she reminded me in her email – so far we've only done two.

We meet in a room at the back of a cafe. The first thing I notice is that her appearance has undergone a transformation – she looks completely different from when I last saw her. I don't know if it's her hair or her glasses or that she's lost or gained weight, but if she hadn't walked into this place and come right over and sat down in front of me, I don't think I'd have known it was her.

The change in her mood is remarkable too. Perhaps the reason I didn't recognise her is that she seems lit up, excited. Sitting up straighter, holding herself differently. Unlike the last time I saw her, she can't seem to stop smiling.

She apologises straightaway for not having sent me anything to read. She says – and she wants me to know that this has never happened to her before – that she finds herself at a stage of her work where she just can't bear to share or show it.

Not to me – not to anyone.

I can't really even tell my boyfriend about it, she laughs.

In fact, though she's brought some pages along with her, she still isn't entirely sure that she wants me to look at them. It isn't that she doesn't trust my judgement. But it's going so well and she feels herself to be so firmly set on a particular course, that she's afraid of doing even the slightest thing to jeopardise it.

It's as if she doesn't want to put herself in a position where someone – not even a writer like me whose work she genuinely respects – might criticise or deflect her or try and tell her it isn't working. Not that it would make any difference really. Because, she says, she's finding that – again, for the first time in her whole life – she doesn't really care what anyone else thinks.

This feeling of knowing exactly what she's doing, of being so completely one hundred per cent excited by what she's writing, well, she's never had that before either.

The only reason I wanted to meet up, she adds as the tea we've ordered is put down in front of us, is because I wanted to tell you all this. To thank you, really. I had to tell someone who I knew would understand. Seriously, you've no idea how happy it's made me.

She smiles at me, and lifting the pot, she pours the tea into both our cups. .

Of course, I'm extremely surprised by all of this. I'd never have dreamed, from our last two meetings, that this rather tentative and closed young woman could ever turn herself around so dramatically. Though I doubt I can take much credit for it. If anything, I'm slightly ashamed, when I remember how ungenerous

I've sometimes been and how little real encouragement I've managed to give her.

But of course, I tell her how delighted I am to hear all of this. I can see just from looking at her face how excited she is. And I assure her that she should definitely just follow her own instincts when it comes to showing it to anyone. I never share my work in progress with anyone, I tell her.

Seriously? she says, looking pleased. Not anyone?

Writing's a balancing act, I tell her. An act of madness, of sustained and necessary obsession, of insane self-belief. The moment you listen to the opinions of others – the moment you even consider letting them in – well then, you risk breaking the spell and, if you're not careful, sanity creeps in.

And – taking all of this in – she looks at me and she laughs and she begins to say something else, only to break off as someone walks past us to go to the toilets. We both watch as the door swings open and shut and we hear the sound of the hand drier going.

Glancing down at the table, she takes a breath.

So, the thing is, I don't know if you remember when I told you before that the novel wasn't autobiographical, that none of the characters were supposed to be me? Well, I wasn't lying. I think at the time I did genuinely believe that. But after our last session, I started thinking: how can I actually be so sure this isn't about me? And once I'd had the thought, well, that was it, I saw the whole thing through new eyes. And all I can say is the entire novel has changed shape in ways that I could never have predicted.

In fact, she continues – in a voice which trembles a little with the effort of telling it – I have to admit that it's ended up being quite a personal piece of work – far more personal than I'd ever dreamed or intended it to be. I'm still a bit shocked, actually, by how far I seem to have been prepared to go on that front. I've said things I didn't even know I felt, let alone dared write. The stuff about my mother, for instance. Well, I guess it's just lucky that she isn't around to read it –

I ask what happened to her mother and she tells me she died quite suddenly, a few weeks ago.

Just after I saw you, actually, she had a massive stroke.

I tell her I'm very sorry to hear that and she shrugs and then she blushes slightly and she tells me it was a shock, of course it was, in fact it still hasn't quite sunk in.

She was a very strong person, very robust, she says. Everyone thought she'd go on forever. I certainly did. I think about her a lot. I loved her, obviously. She wasn't easy, but she'd had a hard life. But I know for a fact that she would have hated this book I'm writing, so –

She breaks off and stares down at the teapot for a moment, fiddling with its metal lid. When she lifts her chin and looks at me, I see tears in her eyes.

I can't believe this novel will ever be published, but at the same time I can't quite believe that it won't be published. It's the weirdest feeling. But in a way none of that matters. What I do know for sure is that I'm going to finish it. I know that it needs to exist. Not just needs to – it does exist –

She smiles at me.

I've never felt so certain about anything before and the feeling is like nothing else. I feel so alive. It's absolutely fucking fantastic.

I DON'T THINK MY MOTHER EVER MEANT to spend her whole life being angry with me. I used to like to tell myself that she did it on purpose – that she got some kind of special satisfaction from all the spite and accusations and point scoring – but I don't believe that now. In fact, I don't think it was ever about anger. I think that all she ever wanted was some love and attention – for people to listen to her, to see her clearly, to understand her for who she was.

Because isn't that all any of us want?

I have an old photograph of my mother, a small sepia picture, mounted and stuck on card. You can tell from the address in the corner that it was taken in a studio. In it she can't be more than three or four years old, dressed in a smart wool coat and little felt hat, her babyish hair curling on her shoulders. And she's clutching a stuffed toy puppy – holding it close up to her face with shining eyes and a smile so wide and uncomplicated – the kind of smile I don't really associate with my mother. She looks as if she loves the puppy so much.

But when I asked her about the picture, she told me it wasn't even hers, that dog. Just a prop that belonged to the studio, she said.

Not long after this photo is taken, my mother is put on a plane and – for reasons which, even many years later, she's unable to explain – sent to that boarding school so many miles away across the sea. It's her father who sends her, but her mother must have agreed to it, she must have let her go.

My mother is five years old and in her bag are two vests, a liberty bodice and two plain cotton dresses, one pink and one blue. She won't go home for a very long time, but she doesn't understand this yet. Every night, she cries herself to sleep. It's a method which, only half-jokingly, she recommends to me later when I'm dealing with your toddler tantrums.

Just put her in her bed and close the door. In the end she'll just exhaust herself, she says.

I don't know whether it's at this school that my mother claims to be a princess and has her mouth washed out with soap and water for lying. I think that might be at the next school, when she's turned into a slender and defiant teenager with a spirit and a smile that will later win over plenty of men, including, I suppose, the man who becomes my father. I know that she's about fifteen when she returns from school for the holidays and runs to find her pet cat, only to be told that her father has had it destroyed. It's soon after this that he takes her out of school and begins insisting she kiss him after breakfast.

WHEN, FINALLY, IN HIS MID-EIGHTIES, MY mother's father dies, she is asked by the undertakers if she wants to see his body and – unsure what to do in such a situation – she agrees to go to view it on the morning of the burial. She asks if I'll go with her, but I tell her I'd rather not. I have you, my six-week-old daughter with me. I am soft, happy, milky. Why would I want to look at a corpse? Isn't it enough that I've driven sixty miles with a new baby to come to the funeral?

Later, though, I feel very bad about this, that I let her go and see her father's body on her own. It's one of so many occasions when I can't – or won't – give my mother what she wants. And it's surely not such a big thing to ask, that I should go with her to look at her father one last time?

On that morning when she goes to see him, my mother and I meet in a cafe by the sea and eat sandwiches while you sleep in your carry-seat at my feet. Even though she's only seen you twice since you were born, she doesn't take much notice of you. Instead she complains about the draught blowing through the cafe and also about the fillings in the sandwiches, prising them apart one by one to see what's inside. She sends her coffee back twice because it isn't hot enough. And she criticises your father for things he apparently did or said several years ago, before telling me I need to start losing my baby weight.

Afterwards she goes outside for a smoke.

When she returns from looking at her father's body, she seems very shaken. She tells me I definitely made the right choice not seeing him, in fact she has no idea why she went. It didn't even look like him, she says, adding with a shudder that she thinks they might have put make-up on him.

They bury my grandfather up on a windy hill, with a one hundred and eighty degree view of the sea. It's a surprisingly lovely place, that cemetery, surrounded as it is by so much water and sky. Because he belonged to so many different evangelical churches, there's a very large crowd, men in black suits with big gold watches, all of them praying and shouting Hallelujahs.

You're asleep in a sling on my chest and just the sensation of your small, warm weight against me is making my breasts prickle. Later, at the wake, I'll find a little chair in an empty room and I'll feed you and it will feel like our own quiet heaven, away from my mother and all the men with their noise and loudness and strong aftershave smells. But for now it's enough to be able to press my lips against the silky top of your head and, as my grandfather's body is lowered into the ground, breathe in its comforting biscuity smell.

The photo of my mother in the coat and hat, holding the toy puppy that belonged to the studio, is on my wall now. It's right here in front of me, as I sit writing this. She clutches the puppy with both small hands and – even though it isn't hers and soon it will be taken away from her and she'll never hold it again – there's such a sweet and mischievous look in her eyes. A look of joy, you'd have to say.

Her face is soft and open in the exact same way your face is at that age. In so many ways, actually, she reminds me of you.

All you want to do is love her.

You just want to put your arms around her and pull her close.

THIS IS DEFINITELY NOT A GHOST STORY. BUT for a while after you're gone, I see you everywhere. Every ragged young person sitting huddled on a pavement, every stretched-out body under cardboard in a shop doorway. In town, outside, walking down the street, everywhere I go, there you suddenly are. Fingers, knees, elbows, the familiar curve of your cheek, the shape of your head. My heart skidding to attention at the sight of your small, neat ears, your white skin. The swish of your long dark ponytail, disappearing down into the gloom of the underpass.

The sound of your voice. The little rise of

surprise when someone tells you something you don't understand.

That laugh of yours, unmistakable.

Especially your laugh.

You once said to me: if ghosts exist, then why don't we see them everywhere – in normal, everyday places like the swimming pool or the shopping centre? Hanging out the washing, lighting a cigarette, sitting at the lights in cars. Frowning into their phones on the corner of some windy street.

But perhaps we do. Because one day I see you going into the newsagent's and coming out a few minutes later with a can. The very next morning, there you are outside the chicken shop. A day later, sitting on the low wall by the tube station and smoking and talking to someone who does not seem to be there.

One startling time, coming down the steps to put the rubbish out, I glance back over my shoulder and for a quick, eerie moment there you definitely are, framed in the cool light of the hallway, just inside our own front door.

A MAN COMES UP TO US ON A TUBE platform. Or he comes up to your father and he asks for money. He has on filthy clothes and his hair is filthy and he has a guitar slung over his back in a dirty nylon case.

Your father shuts his eyes. He tells him to go away.

Just please go, he says in a fierce, angry voice which is startlingly different from his usual voice. I'm not giving you money, so don't ask me, please just leave us alone.

And my heart begins to race because no one's around and the man looks frightening and chaotic, you can tell from the way he holds himself that he has nothing to lose – he's a junkie after all – and it isn't like your father to be so instantly combative and I suppose I'm afraid that the man might do something, that he might hit him or push him or something worse.

I take your father's arm, tightening my grip on him, trying to pull him away. It's a Sunday night. It's late. I wish now that we hadn't come down here to the tube as your father insisted. I wish we'd just taken a taxi home.

And the man puts his face right up close to your father's and he tells him he's a twat, a cunt, just a rich fucking cunt who knows fuck all about anything and he says that he can fuck right off back to his posh fucking life if he wants to.

And then he spits at the ground right next to your father's long, narrow feet in their light-coloured suede boots.

Cunt, he says again, before walking on.

I am shaken.

But, looking at your father through his eyes, I see what he sees. A tall, slender, grey-haired man in a long woollen coat with a too-bright scarf around his neck. Your father isn't young, but you wouldn't call him old either. Certainly he doesn't act his age. His hair's still thick, his eyes steady and intelligent. There do not appear to be any tragedies lurking in those eyes.

Such a smooth and well-fed and privileged face he has. It's very easy to see what assumptions this man might make.

So I wonder what he'd think if he knew that we've just come from the A&E department of the hospital, where we saw you, our daughter – a junkie no different from him – lying on a trolley so used up and near to death (or so it seems to us on that night), tubes strapped to your wrists, dried vomit around your nose and mouth, black crumbs still clinging to your lips where they had to force the charcoal down your throat.

It's the police who call us. Explaining that they have our number logged from the last time you were picked up. No, they don't know what you've taken – some pills apparently – and no, they can't tell us how you are. All they can say is that an ambulance was called. You should be there by now. They give us the name of a hospital on the other side of town.

And your father and I, we know that you're probably OK. We know why you've done this – and we know too that the moment you get what you want, you'll be out of there. It won't be the first time you've done damage to yourself just so that a hospital will be forced to fix you up.

And it's very important that you don't think we'll

come running every time you hurt yourself. You mustn't be allowed to think that swallowing pills is a worthwhile or productive thing to do –

Still, we hurry from the house and rush to the hospital, jumping straight into the first taxi we can find. Rushing so much that we can barely speak. I see the panic in your father's eyes and this frightens me – so does the fact that, for once, he doesn't seem to make the slightest attempt to calm me down. His hands are shaking, he can't think or speak, he tells me he does not know where he's put his keys.

We run in through the glass doors and present ourselves at reception, begging to know whether our child is dead or alive.

The receptionist is in the middle of making herself a mug of tea, carefully squashing the tea bag against the side of the mug with a spoon. Even when we tell her who we are, she continues with this task, removing the bag and, without letting it drip, setting it down on the saucer. And then – so very slowly that I want to grab hold of her hands and do it myself – she puts our details into the computer. After that she gets up and, just as unhurriedly, leads us to where you are lying on a trolley.

Your eyes are shut, your hair pulled off your face. You're fully clothed. It's hard to tell if you're dead or alive.

A nurse comes up and, pulling the curtain round, glances at us kindly and tells us you're going to be all right. Smoothing your hair, lifting your small bloodless hand to check your pulse, she tells us that you're just sleeping. And the alarming ring of black around your mouth is nothing to worry about, just the remnants of the charcoal they've given you, she says.

You're alive. You're just sleeping.

And because of this – because you're all right and don't even know that we're here – there doesn't seem to be any immediate need for us to leave. I look at you, so very hungry for the sight of you. How many months has it been since we last saw you? It is just so good to be able to put my eyes on you and keep them there, with no one around to tell me it's not a good idea.

My baby girl.

I lay my hand on your warm and dirty leg, in the filthy black jeans which you probably haven't changed in weeks. The fabric worn to a furred softness under my fingers, the warmth there so very hard to resist.

I can feel a small pulse, right there in your leg. The blood moving around your body. Good, I think, your heart is working, it works, there's life still in you. I keep my hand on you, let it rest there, letting your body know I'm there. And suddenly I am wildly happy. I can't remember when I was last allowed to touch you like this.

But at last, your father squeezes my hand.

No point in staying, he says. Now that we know she's OK.

He's right. Once you wake, there's nothing we can do to help you. We are both very sure of that. But still I don't move. Keeping my hand on you –

He touches my arm.

Come on, darling.

And so we do it. We turn and we leave. Walking off past reception – past all the sad and properly sick people waiting, past the drinks machines and the stretchers – and out into the black and frightening air outside.

The taste of death thick in our mouths.

It's the hardest thing we ever do for you, leaving you lying there on that hospital trolley and, since there doesn't seem to be any particular hurry any more, getting on the tube and going home.

AT A PARTY, STANDING OUT ON the lawn with the smokers, I get talking to a woman, a writer I've met once before. Almost immediately, she starts telling me all about the book she's writing. Tilting her chin up and blowing smoke into the chilly night air, launching into a surprisingly detailed account of it even though, or so she says, it's still in its early stages.

Strictly speaking, she hasn't even started it yet.

Still, she manages to describe at least half of the plot of this new book to me – where it's set, who the characters are, what exactly inspired it, where she thinks it might be going.

When she starts telling me all this, her voice is light. But as she goes deeper in, allowing me to see more and more of this hidden part of herself, I notice that she slows right down and her face changes. Cigarette in hand, hugging herself and gazing down at the lawn which is trodden to mud. But once she's finished, she's light again – laughing unsteadily and glancing around, as if it's someone else who just stopped speaking.

When I don't immediately say anything, she gives me a sharp look.

You don't like the sound of it, do you? Come on, you can be honest. You don't think it sounds any good.

I tell her it's not that – quite the opposite actually, I think it sounds very impressive. It's just that I'm amazed at her confidence, being able to share so much of it at such an early stage.

I can't talk about my writing to anyone, I tell her. Not until it's completely finished and I've managed to give it a shape that convinces me. And even then I often find it hard to believe that what I've made actually deserves to exist.

For a moment this woman is silent, sucking on her cigarette. At last, lifting her eyes and looking at me, she tells me that she is, it's true, bursting with a new kind of confidence at the moment.

As a writer?

As a writer, yes – but also as a person, a woman, a mother, everything!

She laughs again.

She explains that just under two years ago her husband upped and left her, quite out of the blue, or so it felt to her, for another woman – a younger woman, as if that needed pointing out – who lived a few doors down on the same street.

She says 'husband', but actually she and he never married. They didn't feel the need. They'd been together more than twenty years, bought and sold various houses, had three children together. As he himself said many times, their commitment couldn't have been stronger – why would they need a piece of paper to prove it to the rest of the world?

But within four months of moving in with this other woman, he married her. Apparently this was what she wanted. Or no, scratch that, it was – or so he later very passionately claimed – what he wanted, too, in fact what he'd been wanting all along. For it turned out, or so he said, that in all these so-called happy family years, he'd been lamenting the lack of any real ritual or romance in his life.

So they had a great big wedding, him and this woman, a lavish party, honeymoon, the lot. Now they have eighteen-month-old twins and another one on the way.

Cupping her elbow in her hand, the writer flicks ash off her cigarette and, shaking her head, she flashes me a mournful, lopsided smile.

Of course, she says, all of this was a huge blow to her self-esteem. For a while she felt terrible – old and tired and sad. It didn't help that she was on the verge of menopause. She'd put on weight, her skin was breaking out. Her hormones were going haywire, she was hot all the time, she couldn't sleep. Not only that, but her kids were turning into teenagers – each one with their own different, and differently difficult, problems. There could not have been a worse moment for their dad to run off and start a brand new family.

It affected her work, too. It shocked her to realise that all of her writing had, up to this point, come from a place of such absolute safety and contentment, a state which – she now realises – she'd always taken entirely for granted.

Sure, her novels were known for being dark – and certainly she tried to push herself to less comfortable places – but she just wasn't one of those writers who found creativity in chaos, never had been.

And now all of that safety was gone – finished – it was over. She lay awake in the small hours, hot and miserable and angry, worrying about money, about the house, about her children. Her imagination seemed to be drained, it was empty. All of her former inspiration and attitude seemed to have left her, in fact there were days when she could barely even remember what had compelled her to write fiction in the first place.

What was the point in making up stories when life itself was so dramatic and difficult?

She realised she'd lost all her courage, her ability to put the world at a distance and just get on with it.

She began to wonder if she could even be a writer any more.

I started looking for jobs online, she says. But it was pretty fucking disconcerting. After all, who's going to want to employ a middle-aged novelist with only a smattering of IT skills?

But then, she tells me, something extraordinary happened.

One morning she woke up and – she has no idea why – just knew that something was very different.

Unable to put her finger on exactly what, still, she could sense that there had been a change, a shift. Suddenly, she was acutely aware of herself. By which she means literally that: her own self, the particular fact of her existence. The fact of her own warm body lying there in the bed, her naked, stretched-out limbs, the buzzing weight of her own head.

And not just that, but the reality of the room around her, too – the soft air, the early morning light, the sense of infinite space and also of the rest of her own life out there unwinding like a sheet in the wind, the endless possibility of it –

She breaks off and looks at me and laughs, immediately self-conscious. But then her face grows serious again.

All of her life, she realised, she'd only ever experienced

herself in relation to others. Parents, siblings, husband, children – probably especially children. But now, for the first time, she saw that she was a distinct being, a person answerable to no one. Where she'd previously perceived herself as helpless, she now saw that she wasn't helpless at all – quite the opposite, actually: she was free.

Why had she never understood this before?

And though this realisation might have seemed obvious to anyone else – beyond obvious, stupid more likely – to her it felt just, well, extraordinary. As if all of the rules and restrictions, everything she'd previously imagined to be holding her back, it had all just lifted, whoosh.

And the dark burden of loneliness which had been weighing her down until yesterday – so much so that when her kids were out and she put her key in the door and entered her silent, accusing house, she very often sat herself down in the hall and sobbed – it simply wasn't there any more.

She was alone at last – separate – in the very best possible way. No one telling her what to do or who to be. Even the voices in her head seemed to be silenced.

The sense of liberation was dizzying.

Perhaps even a bit too dizzying. She tells me that in those first few days she experienced the weirdest kind of vertigo. She felt actually physically disoriented sometimes, nauseous and light-headed, as if her entire personality had been excised – as if it had been lifted away and nothing put back in its place – for who exactly was she if not a series of well-worn responses to a set of unquestioned rules?

But slowly, as she got used to this new sensation, she began to realise that her husband had done her a great favour by leaving her. In walking away, he had, whether intentionally or not, removed her safety net – and in doing so, he'd performed the necessary jolt, he'd dislodged the apple, he'd woken her up –

And she could not believe how much happier this had made her.

She sat down immediately and began making notes for this novel.

She smiles at me, taking another suck of her cigarette.

There was so much I'd given up on, so many things I thought I'd never do. In my life, yes, but also in my work. I realised I'd always been writing with a sense of people looking over my shoulder – husband, editor, agent, family, whatever.

It didn't matter who it was, I was always thinking ahead, curbing and filtering myself, wanting so badly to get it right – as if that were possible – so very desperate not to upset anyone, as if I hadn't earned the right to say what I really felt about anything –

I called myself a writer, but, really I was no different from the ten-year-old child I'd once been – lying, spinning, obfuscating, afraid to speak up, terrified of my own voice, so completely uncertain of my right to take up space –

She turns and blinks at me. As if, for a moment or two, she's surprised to find me still standing there. She smiles.

I haven't even asked you what you're writing. But it sounds as if you wouldn't have told me anyway.

I laugh and tell her she's right about that.

But in a way it's not so very different from the story you've just told me, I say.

I AM FOUR YEARS OLD. IT IS hot. I am lying in bed at the end of a long, hot, happy day and listening to the safe sounds of my father emptying the paddling pool out – water whooshing over the grass – and wheeling the tricycles in, my brother's and mine. When he wheels mine in, he rings the bell – a secret sign between us – and in my little bed I thrill and laugh to myself. My tricycle, my daddy.

Now my father is writing a shopping list. He is writing it in blue biro on the back of the evening paper, next to the crossword and the weather forecast. There's whisky on the list. Half a pint of milk. A loaf of white sliced bread. A can of beans.

But he doesn't go shopping. Instead he leaves this list propped next to the kettle on the draining board. Later it is one of the first things that the police will find. That and the note to my brother, with all of its careful underlinings and crossings out.

In the end, it's harder than he expects. Coming in and out of the garage, stumbling, staggering, drunk and poisoned but never quite poisoned enough, grabbing onto the handrail by the back door to get himself back inside –

Until the final day when – having used two large damp bath towels to seal the gaps – this time he manages it and he does not get up. Remaining there at the steering wheel with his two hands on the dashboard. Eventually his face, too, on the dashboard.

First light of dawn at the small window and there he still is, slumped at the wheel of his car. Still sitting in his car, but going nowhere.

My daddy.

Slowly, the day brightens, sun coming up. Bright morning light, a new day. Lunchtime comes and goes. Tea time. Dark again by four.

And my father's neighbour, off to post a letter, notices that the house is unusually dark. Stopping for a moment and wondering. And then because he doesn't want to miss the last collection, walking on.

WHEN YOU AT LAST AGREE – I'D LIKE TO SAY beg, but you've never in your whole life begged us for anything – to come back home for a month in order to clean yourself up in order to go to rehab, we make you stand there in the hall and remove all of your clothes.

Your ripped jacket, your filthy jeans and T-shirt, the grey and sticky-taped trainers that are falling off your feet, the underwear which no longer looks anything like underwear –

You do all of this without a word of complaint. You know that shedding these clothes is a crucial part of the required detox. Standing there by the front door, obedient and unquestioning, lifting your skinny arms and legs as you carefully follow our instructions, doing everything exactly the way we tell you to.

Once every single item of clothing has been dropped into a bin bag, I give you a big, clean bath towel which you wrap around yourself. And then you stand and watch as, opening its grimy flaps one by one, your father and I go through your rucksack. Handing you back your cigarette papers and lighter – as well as a string of light yellow plastic beads which you insist are of sentimental value – but nothing else.

You don't ask us what we're looking for. You don't ask us anything. Apart from telling us about the beads, you are entirely silent throughout this process.

After that, holding the towel around you, you go upstairs for a shower.

SUMMER COMES – ANOTHER SUMMER – AND the weather is dry and warm. And I'm running late, hurrying down a side street to avoid the main road when suddenly there he is, coming out of a shop on the other side. Before I can think about what to do, he's already making his way between the parked cars and coming over to me.

For a moment, everything seems to stop. The city, the bright sunshine, everything. Noise and light and time sucked from the air.

Moving in to kiss me. The look on his face is shocked, delighted, shy.

I wasn't sure it was you, he says. And then, well, when I realised it definitely was, I was afraid you were going to run away from me –

I tell him I would never do that. He laughs, still looking me up and down.

I hope you wouldn't.

I wouldn't.

All right. I believe you.

He laughs again and then he takes a breath, as if he is about to say something else, but he doesn't say it. He goes on looking at me.

This is ridiculous, he says.

Ridiculous?

Running into you again after all these years. I just didn't expect it, that's all.

I ask him how he's been.

Good, he says. I'm good. Very good, actually. What about you?

I tell him I'm fine. And that's when he tells

me – offering it up immediately, as if it's something that must be got out of the way – that he's no longer with his wife.

What? – it's impossible to hide my shock – You mean you split up?

He shrugs.

That's one way of putting it.

For a moment I can't think of anything to say. Then, gathering myself, I tell him how sorry I am – how very sorry.

You don't need to be sorry, he says.

I'm still gazing at him in surprise.

All right, I say. But still, I am.

He lets out a breath.

It happened a long time ago. Eight years ago, to be precise.

Eight years?

Almost nine.

Another moment of silence as I take this in.

Well, I say. I'm just so surprised.

Why? – he tilts his head at me. Why would you be surprised?

I suppose I just thought you two were happy together. Despite everything. You always told me you were happy.

A look goes over his face.

I doubt I ever said that.

All right. But still. I thought you were.

He hesitates.

If it makes you feel any better, it had nothing to do with you.

It didn't?

No. In the end she just gave me an ultimatum.

An ultimatum about what?

He looks down at the pavement.

I don't know. Everything, really.

I tell him again that I'm sorry. And that's when he tells me, rushing the words as if he's afraid of them, that he got married last year, to someone he used to work with.

We have a baby girl, he says, raising his eyebrows as if this fact is still surprising, even to him.

I stare at him, my face suddenly hot.

You do?

He nods. His eyes are steady. He bites his lip – and something about the way he does it makes me notice for the first time that, though the hair at his temples is still barely grey, his face is old.

We do, yes.

When I congratulate him, he pulls a face.

The trouble is she wants more – can you believe it? – I think she wants at least two kids, maybe three. But I'm honestly not sure I want to go down that route again.

It might be fun? I say.

He laughs and shakes his head.

I'm sorry, no, too old, too tired – and what about you, how's your little girl doing? She must be a big girl now.

I tell him my daughter's fine – on a gap year, travelling all over the place.

I haven't seen her in months, I say. Well, it feels like months anyway.

You must miss her.

I do, I say. I do miss her.

I take a breath.

And suddenly – or perhaps it's not all that sudden – I'm aware of the traffic again, the people all around us, the relentless life of the city with its tall grey buildings and the wide sky and the sun, the hot summer sun, which had briefly disappeared behind clouds but is blazing again.

I tell him I have to get on.

He looks at me.

Why?

I'm meeting someone.

What, for lunch?

Yes, lunch.

A lunch date – he tries to smile – Lucky guy.

What makes you think it's a man?

Is it a man?

It's not a man, no.

He smiles again. He doesn't ask me who I'm meeting. Blinking at me in the sunshine.

I still read everything you write, you know.

You do? I say, genuinely surprised.

Of course I do. I still think about you. I still dream about you, if you really want to know. And reading you is the only way I have of knowing what's going on in that head of yours.

For a moment I don't know what to say to this. When I point out to him that my novels are purely fiction, he laughs and nods.

Yes, he says. Yes of course. Fiction. It's very clever what you do, hiding in plain sight like that.

I tell him I don't know what he means.

I think you do.

I feel my face grow hot again. And then I tell him the truth – that I haven't written anything in a while.

I haven't been very productive lately, I say. I've slowed right down –

But he isn't listening.

All I would ask, he says, is that you don't ever write about me.

I tell him I wouldn't dream of it.

OK. I believe you. Just thought I should check.

And he smiles, telling me again how good it is to see me and taking hold of my hand and squeezing it.

Still so beautiful, he says, holding onto my hand. Look at you, pretty lady. My god, I've missed that face, you've no idea how I've missed it. We should catch up properly, you and me, have a drink one of these days.

I tell him we should. But it is noticeable that he doesn't ask me for my number.

As we say goodbye, I ask him how his boys are. For a moment the light drops out of his eyes.

My boys?

Yes, I say. They must be almost grown up now. How are they? Are they OK?

He lifts his head and gives me a long look.

No one's ever really OK, are they? But we do our best.

A PHOTOGRAPHER – A WOMAN I HAVEN'T known very long – asks me if she can take my picture. She's making a series of photographs celebrating women of a certain age, she says, and she'd like to include me. It isn't anything to do with my being a writer, she adds. It's just a celebration of real women and their real lives – their beauty and resilience and strength. She says it will probably only appear online. Though you never know, she might make a book of it later.

I already know this woman's work. I'm too shy to say it, but almost as soon as I met her, I subscribed to her blog. Each time she posts a new picture, I give it my whole attention, scrutinising every sweep and line and shadow, looking and looking for something, I don't know what.

The women she photographs aren't young – far from it. Often well past middle age, and shown very much unadorned, dressed in loose clothes and standing barefoot in empty rooms, their open faces – freckled, laughing, often without make-up – turned towards the light. Each picture comes with a brief paragraph of text written by the woman herself. Who she is and how she sees herself and how she feels about being photographed, where exactly she is in her life, what lies behind her and what might be ahead –

And naturally these lives are far from perfect – they're strewn with all the sadnesses and losses and difficulties that you might expect. And yet despite, or perhaps because of, this – as well as thanks to the frank generosity of this photographer's vision – each picture is beautiful in exactly the same way. As if each of these women has been captured at a time of perfect balance and candour in her life – neither cowed nor apologetic or afraid to take up space. Sure, each one seems to be saying, this happened, or that happened, life isn't perfect – but, so what, who cares, here I am.

Even though she's beginning to be a friend, this photographer only really knows one side of me. I've been careful to see to that. So I can understand why she might imagine that I'm one of these women. From the outside, anyway, I'm sure there are plenty of reasons why a person might think that.

So it's with a certain amount of shame that I tell her I can't do it. I'm flattered to be asked, I say, but she's wrong about me, I don't have what these women have. Her photographs are all about what's on the inside and I am a ghost, a blur, devoid of substance or heart. There is nothing real in me, nothing substantial or solid. Nothing that would show up in a photograph anyway.

MY MOTHER'S GRAVE IS EXACTLY where my brother said it would be, just off to the left of the gravel drive that leads up to the little shingled church. It's only been three months, but still it looks newer than I expected, the squares of turf still barely fused together, the mound uneasily human in shape.

As if my mother's just under there sleeping and might at any moment get up and toss the covers off.

Though I don't think that she is sleeping.

In life and all through my childhood, my mother moved house constantly, seeming to require a complete change of surroundings every few years. She loved houses – buying them, doing them up. But once each place was finished, we'd be packing up and moving on, we probably never lived more than three years in one place. So it's very hard to believe that this silent, ancient churchyard is where she'll now stay forever.

Still, my mother would be the first person to say she isn't here – don't bother visiting my grave, she used to say. But for the first time in a long time, she doesn't feel very far away. There isn't a headstone yet. Just a small wooden sign with her name on. I didn't think I'd cry but as soon as I see that little sign, the tears come.

After I've laid the flowers, I take a picture of the

grave with my phone. I do briefly worry about this – is it all right to photograph a grave? But later, on the train home, I'm very glad to have this picture. I look at it for a long time, stretching it with my finger and thumb, blowing it up bigger and bigger until all I can see are the bright green blades of grass growing over the place where my mother lies.

SOON AFTER THE INCIDENT WITH THE MAN in the tube station, your father is on his way out of the house when he sees someone trying to steal a bike from the racks at the end of our road. Cutting through the lock at six in the evening, with plenty of people walking by. And without a second thought, he shouts at the man to stop what he's doing, but before he can say anything else, the man turns around and punches him. Hitting him hard in the face with his fist before running off down the road.

The blow doesn't knock him over. But by the time someone comes to the house to fetch me, he's sitting on the pavement with his head in his hands.

Both the man and the bike have gone.

Your father tells me he's fine, but he doesn't look fine. He says he doesn't remember the moment of being hit. He doesn't remember much, actually. And the police come and they take a statement and then, despite your father's protests, they insist on taking us to the hospital.

The doctor who checks him over says he's fine, but he tells us to watch out over the next few hours for any signs of concussion.

Your father's very quiet as we leave the hospital. He doesn't speak or make jokes as he normally would and I notice that he walks very slowly. Holding onto my arm as we go down the ramp and make our way onto the main road to find a taxi to go home.

And when the taxi driver asks us if we've been out anywhere nice for the evening, we can't help it, we laugh and then we tell him the truth: that we just spent the last four hours in A&E. And when we tell him why, he looks very surprised and says that he takes his hat off to my husband, having a go at a thief in the street like that – he isn't so sure that he'd have the bottle to do it himself.

And then, keeping his eyes on us in the mirror, he says exactly the same thing that the police said. That he's in no doubt whatsoever that the man was a junkie. He was bound to be, wasn't he, stealing a bike in broad daylight like that?

It's beyond belief, isn't it, he says as he flicks the indicator to turn left into our road, what lengths those people will go to in order to get a fix.

THE YOUNG WOMAN I'VE BEEN teaching sends me her book. She says it didn't take her long, in the end, to finish it. Once she found her momentum, once she got rid of all the rubbish and chit-chat and fakery and worked out exactly where it was that she was going with it, well, then it was almost as if she could feel herself galloping towards the finish line (apologies for the clunky metaphor, she says, but my brain is just so fucking tired).

Fitting the writing in around her day job, she got on and worked every hour she possibly could, sometimes getting herself to her desk by five or six in the morning, so she could fit in a couple of hours before work. She wrote seven or eight drafts in the end, pruning and honing it, managing, she hopes, to be a little bit tougher on herself with each rewrite.

She got it down to roughly a quarter of its original size in the end.

And now that she's finished, she's feeling rather drained.

I don't think I come out of it very well, she says. I'm sure it's much too frank in places. I've been open about all sorts of things I probably shouldn't have been open about.

But the most exciting news of all is that the book's been taken on by an agent and there's already been some interest from a publisher (possibly even two publishers, though she's trying not to think about that). And of course, she's more thrilled about this than she could ever have imagined. Petrified too, though. She says I'll probably understand the reason for her terror when, or if, I can find the time to read it.

Because the thing is, even though the book's most definitely a novel, she has to admit that – as she might have mentioned when we met in the cafe – she's taken some risks with it. Some of its content is, at least loosely – or perhaps even occasionally not so loosely – inspired by certain events within her family. When she says 'inspired by', what she means is that, although every single one of the characters is absolutely and entirely fictional, she kept on finding herself bouncing off real things, real emotions, real events – certain significant moments from her own real life – and in the end it all just felt so right that she just stopped worrying about the consequences.

Though not everything in the novel is real, of course.

She wouldn't want anyone to think that.

Most of what she's written is pure fiction.

Or perhaps it's more accurate to say that it's a kind of fiction which could not possibly have been written were it not for the real things that have happened to her in her real life. But then isn't that true of almost all novels at the end of the day?

And when she says she's stopped worrying about the consequences, she doesn't quite mean that. Of course she's worried! But it does all the same seem to her to be a very benign and careful, and possibly even loving, piece of work – or at least she really hopes it comes over that way. She's been surprised, actually, at how just the simple act of writing it seems to have made her feel kinder and better-disposed towards certain members of her family.

I don't go along with the idea of writing as therapy, she says. But it's weird how much calmer and lighter I feel. Almost as if I've written my way to some kind of a rapprochement, or at least an understanding of sorts.

Though I can't be sure that anyone else will see it that way, of course.

Finally, she wants to tell me that she had no idea, when she first met me, about everything that had happened with my daughter. And of course she understands why I might have wanted to keep it private. But now that she does know, well, she hopes I won't mind if she tells me how very sorry she is.

Not being a parent herself, she can't begin to imagine what it feels like. But, having had a cousin who struggled for years with such things, she does at least have an understanding of how much misery it brings on families. She adds that she perhaps ought to warn me that her book does slightly touch on this subject. She hopes I won't find it too upsetting to read.

SOMETIMES, IF YOU ASK YOUR FATHER a question he doesn't like, he'll stare into the distance for a very long time and say nothing. And you can wait for as long as you like, but a response is unlikely to come. And then at last, if you press him, he'll take a little breath and, as if he considers it very unreasonable to be forced to speak when he'd far prefer to remain quiet, he'll tell you he doesn't know what you want him to say.

And this is what happens when I try to ask him about the time when we're in a restaurant with some friends and some people that they know come up to our table. And one of these people is a tall and striking young woman with platinum blonde hair and wide, athletic shoulders and, as she approaches us, they tell us that she's a musician, a singer, quite a well-known one apparently.

And when she's introduced to us, I notice that she and your father barely greet each other. Instead they exchange no more than a glance – a single glance that makes my stomach drop – and then, a little too quickly, she turns away.

And much later, as we sit at home with the lights off and the TV paused and a glass of wine in our hands, I ask him what it was that happened.

What do you mean, what happened?

Back then. With the musician woman. When she came up to our table. The way you looked at each other. It was weird. Almost as if you knew each other.

And your father says nothing. He stares straight ahead of him at the TV where the man on the news is still frozen, his eyes closed, in the middle of his sentence.

He sips his drink.

Well? I say.

Well what?

Well, do you know her?

But your father still says nothing. He does not answer me. And then, when he's been sitting there in silence for some time – possibly as long as a couple of minutes – he turns to me and he tells me that he does not know what I want him to say.

MY MOTHER IS ILL AND HAS TO go into hospital for an operation and because there are complications, she ends up being in there for some time. At first, when we think it will only be a week or so, she lets me visit her. But once they've broken it to her that she's going to be kept in longer, she tells me she doesn't want any more visitors. When I press her, she tells me, with tears in her voice, that she doesn't want to be remembered like this, all frail and sick and sorry for herself.

I tell her that she doesn't seem at all sorry for herself.

I'd just rather get through this on my own, she says.

So I don't visit. Instead I try to do some of the things that any normal, loving daughter might do. I send her encouraging cards and texts. I don't send flowers because they aren't allowed on the ward, but I look out for little presents – a hand cream, a lip balm – as well as books that I think she might like. Nothing too taxing or depressing, just various soulful family dramas with wistful yet upbeat endings.

My mother thanks me for the books, but says she can't

find it in her to read at the moment. Even listening to the radio feels a bit too much. Most of the time, she says, she just likes to lie there with her eyes closed. But aren't I lucky, she adds. I'll have all these lovely books to look forward to when they let me go back home.

Meanwhile, we continue to talk on the phone. In fact – and I admit this surprises me – I find I'm talking to her far more easily and more regularly than I have in a long time. All of the coldness seems to have vanished from her voice. I don't feel that she's waiting to attack me for every single thing I say. Our chats are almost cosy – now and then we even share a joke. I forgot that my mother could laugh like that. Sometimes – often, actually – I hear myself telling her that I love her when we say goodbye.

I love you too, my darling, she says, and for once, she sounds as if she means it, in fact I'm startled by the genuine warmth in her voice.

And I didn't think I'd ever have it in me to be so nice to my mother, but it turns out not to be very hard at all. I wake up most mornings thinking of her, imagining her in that high, metal hospital bed with the TV angled up above her and the nurses and doctors doing their rounds. And I picture her lying there all alone and find myself wondering how she's feeling and, without even having to think very much about it, I reach for my phone and send her an affectionate text.

She tells me how she appreciates these little messages of mine, how much they comfort and cheer her. She says she doesn't blame him, because she knows how busy he is, but my brother hasn't been in touch with her very much – he hasn't visited at all, she tells me, not even at the beginning.

But he doesn't really like hospitals, she says.

Meanwhile, she often has pain and doesn't have much of an appetite. The doctors are still concerned about her – the wound from the operation isn't healing well – and often she becomes very sad, dwelling on the past in a morose way, certain, all of a sudden, that she's going to die in that place.

One morning she rings me very early, in tears, and tells me I must promise her that when she goes I'll plant a cherry tree. A winter cherry, with the sweetest pink blossom, she says, something to remember her by.

I tell her not to be so silly. Of course she isn't going to die.

And when I suggest to her that her low mood might be due to a lack of visitors – for it surely isn't good for anyone to lie there all alone in hospital for so long? – she insists that she really is much better on her own. She reminds me that boarding school prepared her for experiences like this. It was very character-building, being sent away like that. Among other things, it taught her how to cope with loneliness. And when she talks like this, I remember the little girl in the photograph holding on with such joy to the toy puppy which doesn't even belong to her and I have to swallow back tears.

During all those weeks that my mother is in hospital – for she's quite seriously ill and in the end is stuck there for at least a couple of months – my relationship with her is gradually transformed. More than once she asks me how your father is, and actually sounds interested in hearing the answer. And when, for the first time ever, she asks me how things are with you and, after only the briefest hesitation, I tell her the truth – for in those days the news is never very good – she seems able to listen without blaming or chastising or telling me what we should or shouldn't be doing to handle you.

One time when we're talking about you, she suddenly tells me that she feels very sorry for me – for both of us as parents. She hates to think about all the pain and sadness and anxiety we've endured and she wishes there'd been more she could have done to help us all. And just hearing her say this feels comforting in ways I could never have imagined.

In fact, during this period that my mother is in the hospital, everything about me seems to change, to lighten. Even your father remarks on it. He says that I seem less anxious, less tired, less troubled. As if a burden I hadn't even known I was carrying has been lifted off me.

And it's true.

I am light.

I'm someone's daughter – why wouldn't I be light?

It's a fact which so many people in the world take

for granted, but it's never occurred to me before. The strength and confidence that comes from being loved by a parent, it's astonishing – I suppose I've never given it any thought. But now I find myself glancing at ordinary, happy-looking people in the street – people whose parents probably love them and have always loved them, people who can take it for granted that they're cared for – with a new kind of respect.

No wonder you're all smiling, I think.

I develop a whole new kind of energy, a brand new enthusiasm for the world. I find myself laughing out loud at jokes on the radio, eating my supper hungrily, taking the stairs two at a time. For the first time in a very long time, I'm able to watch TV programmes and read magazine articles about mothers and daughters without feeling numb or stressed or sad.

If someone mentions their own mother, I nod encouragingly. Yes, I want to say, me too. In shops, I keep on noticing things I'd like to buy for my mother, objects that remind me of her, silly things that I just know she'd like.

One time – for this is the middle of December – I spot some glass baubles that I think she'd enjoy putting on her tree when she comes out of the hospital. And even though they aren't cheap, I buy them for her right there on the spot, my heart almost bursting with happiness as I tell the girl who puts them into the special, tissue-lined box that they're for my mum.

Christmas is coming and I have a mum.

It's a crazy thing for a middle-aged woman to go around thinking, but a part of me just wants to shout it out to every person I see.

WHEN I TRY TO ASK YOU ABOUT your new boyfriend, you tell me he isn't your boyfriend, you don't want me thinking that. Just someone you met in rehab, you say – clean now, clean in fact for a whole lot longer than you've been clean.

He's been living out of the city for a while, staying up north with friends, but you've kept in touch and now he's back, he doesn't know for how long, but for a while anyway. But the two of you aren't in any kind of relationship. You're just hanging together, you say.

When I ask you what this boy does for a living, you don't look happy. Ever since you gave up the job at the charity shop, it's been in your interest to try and persuade me that work isn't compulsory for people in their twenties. You've told me again and again that most people's parents don't expect their adult kids to have a job. Most of them still live at home, just as you do. Rent is practically unaffordable, you remind me, even for people who haven't had the problems that you've had.

Actually, you say, this friend of yours is kind of hoping to make it as a musician. He plays bass and writes songs and has already had some success with his own stuff at open mic sessions. But for now, he's just holding it together and going to meetings and working some shifts at the fried chicken place.

That's impressive, I tell you, that he has a job, I mean.

Only part-time.

All the same.

I'm actually even more impressed that he gets himself to meetings, but I know better than to tell you that. You know exactly how desperately your father and I wish you would go to regular meetings, instead of claiming, as you do, that you're a new and unique kind of addict, a person who is above such things.

There's not a single second of a single day when I ever take your sobriety for granted. I will never stop reminding myself that it hangs by a thread.

You tell me that you're going to have to go in a minute. You're off to see someone who might pay you to walk their dogs and you don't know how long it's going to take you to get there.

OK, I say.

And I wait for you to leave, but you don't leave –

Sitting there and – just as you used to when you were younger and we'd all sit around the supper table laughing and arguing – breaking the long solid drips of wax off the big, white candle and crumbling them on the kitchen table.

For a moment we both watch your two hands working away, breaking the wax into smaller and smaller pieces.

At last you sigh. You tell me that, even if you wanted this boy to be your boyfriend – and you definitely don't – you aren't actually sure that you're strong enough for a relationship yet.

I ask why you need to be strong.

You lift your head and look at me.

Well, what if it fucks you up? What if your heart gets broken?

So what if it does?

A shadow goes over your face.

I'm not sure I'd want the pain of that, you say.

Pain. Something inside me grows small and quiet.

But that's how you grow, I tell you. It's how your soul grows. You get to know someone and you open yourself up and you allow them in and I suppose that, yes, along the way, you do run the risk of a little bit of pain –

Or a lot of pain?

I hesitate.

Sometimes, yes, a lot of pain.

You blow out air, shaking your head.

It can't be worth it –

Oh, but it is.

But all that stuff – I mean, getting so fucked up?

I promise you it is.

And you look down at the table and I see that, even though you look like you're concentrating very hard on the candle, you're also listening to me.

You really believe that? you say, as you break off another piece of wax.

I take a breath.

I have to believe it. We all do.

And you turn then, and you give me a long, hard look. And I tell myself that this might be it, the moment when I have to let you ask about your father and me. And I know that if you do that – and this is something I've thought about so many times – I'll have to try my best to be honest. I won't lie or obfuscate or cloud things in an attempt to protect myself. I'll be frank about what happened – I won't try and show myself in a good light. However shameful it feels, I know how important it is to be straight with you.

But you don't ask me anything. Instead you're quiet. Sweeping all the crumbs of wax off the table, holding them there in the palm of your hand.

My counsellor says I should be very careful, you know. About relationships.

Does she?

Yes, she does. She says they might be a trigger for me.

I bite my lip.

Isn't everything a trigger?

What do you mean, everything?

Well, isn't life a trigger?

You flick a look at me.

Yes, but relationships are a serious trigger. If they go wrong, I mean. Baby steps, that's what she says.

And we both know that by choosing to mention your counsellor like that, you're pulling away from me again and gently – or perhaps not so gently – reminding me that already in your life you've had to rely on help and guidance from people other than me, your mother.

This is a fact which causes me pain every time I think about it. That and the fact that for a brief and hardly ever discussed period of time, you more than on one occasion slept on the streets.

I tell you that actually, whether he's your boyfriend or not, I like this friend of yours, I really do, I like him a lot.

There's just something about him, I say. He seems very kind.

And you look at me with bright eyes, then, unable to hide the pleasure on your face.

Yes, you say. He is. I think that too. I thought it the moment I met him, actually.

I ask you where he's from.

From?

Where was he born?

And you laugh and roll your eyes, losing interest now. Picking up your phone.

I don't know, you say. I haven't asked him. Just somewhere in the north, I suppose.

I don't ask you how old he is. I suspect that when it comes to questions, I've already pushed my luck. But you tell me anyway. You tell me that he's younger than you – a couple of years younger, actually. Still in his teens. But he has a kid, you say, as if that changes things, which of course in some crucial way, it does.

Surprised, I ask you if he gets to see much of his child.

You hesitate. A look I can't decipher crosses your face.

I don't know, you say. I've been afraid to ask him very much about it, actually. I don't want to push it. It's complicated. I think it makes him sad.

And as you get up from the table and go over to the bin to brush the wax off your hands, I realise that, for the first time in as long as I can remember – ever, possibly – I just heard you worry about someone else's feelings, someone else's pain.

This is what she's like, I think. My daughter. She's a good girl. She cares about people, and she's kind.

Very kind.

And it's indescribable, how much pleasure this realisation gives me.

THERE'S A PHOTO I KEEP IN THE TOP left-hand drawer of my desk, a little picture in an old lacquered frame. I used to have it out on my desk, but not any more.

In the photo, you're very young – only one or two years old – and I'm holding you in my arms and we're standing on a hot beach with the sun shining down on us, sea glittering behind us, sky so blue above. My bikini is the brightest neon pink. I remember that bikini. You're wearing nothing, your plump legs wrapped around my hip, your small hand pressed against my breast. And my ponytail's slick and dark from the sea, your hair too, a couple of wet curls on the top of your little head. And I'm looking at you and you're looking back at me, the two of us looking at each other and laughing.

And we're still just babies, both of us.

Nothing has happened to us yet.

IT'S NOT THAT I THINK THE BODY IN the sleeping bag on the church steps could be you. There's no longer any chance of that. But it's still very hard, as I stand here at the window watching the black sleet come down, not to let the thought go through my mind.

It's the middle of winter – dark by three o'clock – the air empty, icy, raw. And the sleeping bag, surrounded as it is by so many cardboard boxes, empty food cartons and plastic carrier bags, has to be soaking wet by now. Sometimes all of these things blow around the church car park, only to be gathered up again and placed, not always effectively, under a brick which is kept there for the purpose. Other times, when the person has disappeared for a while – presumably to use a toilet or get a fix – they just blow around.

And this person – it's hard, because of the hood, to tell if it's a man or woman – always sleeps with their shoes off. Even during the fiercest winter cold and wet, he or she removes them at night. I know this because

I've often stood at the window in the morning and watched him or her waking and sitting up and looking around and then reaching to put their trainers back on.

Sometimes I've even found myself going over to the window the moment I wake up, just so that I can see this happen.

One night two other people come and join this person. I can tell from the voices that at least one of them is female. Three of them, then, sitting on the steps, talking and shouting until late in the evening. And the shouting eventually grows louder – one of the people gets up and starts to stagger around, throwing their hands in the air and shouting angrily.

It sounds like some kind of an altercation to me. Worried that a fight might be about to break out, I ask your father if we should call the police.

The look on his face tells me that he has no idea what I'm talking about. He smiles at me, says I needn't worry. He's sure, he says, that all they're doing is shooting the breeze and having fun.

The noise goes on until well past midnight.

But your father must be right, because in the morning, there's just the one body again, wrapped up in the sleeping bag and huddled against the pale stone pillars of the church, and next to it the trainers, removed and placed as usual on a sheet of newspaper.

*

SO WHAT ABOUT YOU? YOU say, frowning as you scroll through the messages on your phone.

What about me?

Well, what are you doing? For work, I mean. Are you writing something?

Now I'm startled. I don't think you've ever once in your whole life asked me about my work.

I don't know, I tell you. Possibly. It's hard to say.

Why is it hard to say?

And I do think, then, about telling you the truth. That I haven't been able to write for some time, that for some reason I don't understand, the words don't light each other up as they used to. That I go through the motions but feel compelled – endlessly – to delete and delete, judging and scraping away, censoring myself until all meaning is gone.

The crazy lightness I used to have is gone – I can't seem to build anything from nothing any more.

Nothing I can believe in, anyway.

And I am ashamed of how deeply my ego seems to have been affected by this fact.

A few days ago, I read a proof of a new novel by a friend of mine – staying awake into the small hours to finish it, unable to sleep or think until I'd got myself through to the end – and afterwards, when I'd finished, I wept.

Because it was so precisely and perfectly imagined. But also because its right to exist was so absolutely unquestionable. More than anything, it felt so completely and unassailably necessary.

The thing is, I tell you now. I'm not even sure I can be a writer any more.

This gets your attention. Looking up from your phone.

Fuck's sake. But what on earth else would you be?

I don't know, darling. I've honestly no idea.

You stare at me.

You can't not be a writer. Come on, it's the whole thing about you, it's what you do, it's who you are.

I can't help it, I laugh. But at the same time, I think: she doesn't know anything about me at all.

I can't write if I have nothing to say, I tell you.

You pull a face. Looking up from your phone where you seem to be writing a text.

Come on, you have a shitload to say.

I shrug.

It doesn't always feel that way.

Write about this, then. Write about your own life – your real fucking life. Write about dad going off with someone and having a baby –

Hmm, I say. I'm not sure I'd want to do that –

Why not?

I don't think he'd like it very much.

You put your phone in your pocket, slide your legs off the bench.

Well, but you have a right, don't you? You experienced it. Isn't it your thing just as much as his?

I hesitate.

Just because you experienced something doesn't mean you can write about it. And anyway I just wonder if it's time to do something else with my life, that's all.

But you're over fifty! It's too late to do something else –

Thanks.

Only joking.

No, you weren't, but I love you anyway.

You get up to go. You look happy, your cheeks flushed. I wonder if it's your friend, the one who isn't a boyfriend, that you've been texting.

All right, you say. But I don't like to think of you not writing. I've literally no fucking idea what else you'd do.

YOU ARE BORN FAST, VERY FAST, nothing like the first babies I've read about. Just four quick hours, so quick and efficient that the midwife laughs. I think this baby knows what she's doing, she says. I think she's done it all before.

When it's all over, it's still the middle of the night and your father goes home to get some sleep and fetch the little padded seat for the car – and you and me, we lie awake together in the hospital ward with the hushed night sounds going on around us.

Cradling you in one arm, I reach out with the other and I peel a banana, the best banana I've ever eaten, devouring it bite by slippery bite. And you look at me and I look at you, the white blanket wrapped tight around your slick newborn body, your furious black eyes staring out –

Once or twice, the midwife comes in to check on you. But seeing you still so tight and snug in my arms, she smiles. Saying she doesn't even need to check your temperature – not if I'm keeping you warm like that, she says – and out she goes, leaving us alone together again.

And I feel so very proud of myself then, for being such a good mother, for keeping you warm.

We keep our eyes on each other. You can't smile yet. You can't do anything. I can't do anything either. All I can do is try and keep you warm.

I RUN INTO AN OLD FRIEND, SOMEONE I haven't seen in a long time. It has to be fifteen years, more probably. But I recognise her straightaway. She looks exactly as she used to in the days when you and her daughter went to judo classes together. And she's just come out of a store that your father and I used to love going into, back in the days when it didn't seem at all strange to spend an afternoon shopping for pretty things.

And after she's greeted me and given me a hug, this woman tells me how she just met up with her daughter for lunch – the daughter who, she's quick to tell me, got married last year and is due any day now. And they went into the store afterwards to try and find something for the baby, but came out with nothing, in fact they both agreed that the place was nothing like as good as it used to be, overpriced, and full of so many things you just didn't need –

And as she spills all of this out to me, I see the expression in her eyes slowly change, the breath beginning to leave her as the horror dawns –

Blushing hard, she lays a hand on my arm. Apologising profusely. Telling me how devastated she is – how she just did not think – how very often, over these past years, she's thought about me and wondered how I am.

She almost wrote to me at the time, she says. She should have written to me – again and again she thought about doing it. She apologises again for going on about her girl.

I feel absolutely terrible, she says.

And I smile at her, touch her on the arm. I want to hug her. Perhaps I do hug her. I tell her it's fine.

Really, I say, I don't mind hearing about other people's children. It isn't horrible at all, quite the reverse, it gives me a lot of pleasure actually, to hear all the stories, to know how everyone has got on.

And this is almost true.

It is.

It almost does.

As we say goodbye, we hug again and I wish them good luck with the baby.

*

MY MOTHER WAS RIGHT ABOUT ME. She is right. Because the terrible thing about writers – the thing that singles them out from all the other normal and careful and decent people – is that whatever happens to them, however many painful and unexpected and frightening things, and however much they might stand to lose by describing them, it doesn't stop them –

Nothing stops them. Nothing. Once they've started, that's it – they'll go to any lengths to find the right words.

I told you I wasn't sure I could be a writer any more – that I doubted I had anything left to say.

But it wasn't true.

It isn't true.

It's never really true, is it?

BECAUSE I DO HAVE THIS ONE IDEA. I DON'T know if it's fiction or nonfiction. I think I'm still a little afraid of it. I haven't dared write a word of it yet –

There's this couple, you see – a man and woman – who, for a very long time now, have been living a life of despair, unable to do anything to help their only child, a daughter.

It's a dead kind of life they've been living. Occasionally, it's true, they manage some normal things. They'll go shopping, do the garden, cook dinner, drink a glass of wine, now and then they might even manage to make love. They don't see friends, because the friends, understandably perhaps, fell away long ago.

They still work of course – he still has his job, the mortgage still has to be paid – but for her, it isn't easy. You need a free mind to be a writer, a light and surprisingly unencumbered mind and, inevitably perhaps, her mind just isn't that free any more. Sometimes she envies him his long and purposeful days at the office. Her life no longer feels useful or purposeful; she hasn't managed to write anything that feels properly alive in a long time.

Last time they saw their daughter – some months ago now – she came to the house and she sat right there on that sofa in the sitting room and she told them she'd just used. She was admitting it, she said, because she was ready to give up now. This was the absolute last time. She really meant it. It was very important, she said, that they believed her about this.

And they listened to her – they always listen to her – but they were cautious, too, of course they were, they didn't get their hopes up, they were almost ashamed of how cautious they were. Watching as she walked off down the street, turning at the very last moment and giving them a bright little wave –

Just as if she was going to be back later.

But she wasn't back later.

She wasn't.

She isn't.

And then one night the mother wakes up out of a deep sleep with such a feeling of dread that she hears herself cry out. Her husband is used to this. Putting his hand on her head, touching her neck, soothing her back to sleep. The soft warm weight of his hand – it works every time.

She sleeps until morning.

It will haunt her forever, that she manages to sleep that night.

But the next day – even though she knows she is being ridiculous – she persuades her husband that they should drive to their daughter's flat, the squalid and run-down place they've only ever been into that one time when they moved her in, and which, much against their better judgement, they've been paying for all this time.

The flat's on a windy, dirty main road above a newsagent's, the kind of road you only ever drive down to get to somewhere else. When they bang on the door and get no answer, they go into the shop and ask the landlord for the key. And the landlord isn't at all happy. Standing there behind the counter and looking these parents up and down. Their nice coats, their polite and level voices, their soft, clean hair.

His tenant has been nothing but trouble ever since she came, he says. He is thinking of giving her notice, if they really want to know. He doesn't like the types who visit her, folk he'd rather not have around his place. And he mentions the smell of refuse that always comes from the flat. People have commented on it, several neighbours have complained. He's afraid that if it goes on it will attract rats.

They apologise to this man and tell him they'll look into it. And he hands them the key and they go back up the shaky iron fire escape and at the top they unlock the cheap thin door and go in – sure enough, the smell is terrible, it's hard to ignore – and there, just as they've been expecting and fearing and dreading for longer than they can remember, they find her.

She's lying close to the edge of the bed, on filthy sheets that are spotted and streaked with blood. She's wearing a T-shirt and a pair of knickers, nothing else. One trainer is on and the other off. The plastic handle of a supermarket carrier has been used as a tourniquet and the needle is still in your arm. Next to you on the floor, cold and apparently uneaten, is a carton containing some chicken and fries.

And part of your face is hidden by the pillow, but the part we can see is surprisingly tranquil and untroubled. Your eyes are closed, your cheeks soft, there's even the smallest hint of a smile on your lips.

You look calm, satisfied.

At peace, almost –

You look as if you have exactly what you want.